See! The magic of the moonlight
Links each star to twinkling star;
And the velvet air of evening
Brings sweet dreams of Vàldovar.
So if you would be a Dreamer,
You must quickly lay your claim
To this book and to its stories,
By inscribing here your name:

Now record when you received it.
(Keep your writing neat and clear!)
Note the day:

The month,

and, lastly,
Don't forget to write the year:

Dreams of
Vàldovar

For
Lily, Katie and Alexander

Dreams of Vàldovar

by

Neil Johnson

Illustrated by

Victoria Flack

Marius Press

Marius Press Publishers
Box 15, Carnforth LA6 1HW, UK

A CIP catalogue record for this book is available from the British Library

ISBN-13: 978-1-871622-27-0
ISBN-10: 1-871622-27-1

Typesetting by The Drawing Room Design Ltd, Over Kellet, Lancashire, UK.
Colour origination by Graphic Reproductions (Morecambe) Ltd, Morecambe, Lancashire, UK
Printed and bound by The Bath Press, Bath, UK

Contents

The Lost Book of Vàldovar

Following the publication of *Magic in Vàldovar*, I have been asked many times "How do you know so much about events that occurred such a long time ago, and in a country lying far, far across the sea?" Well, I think it is time I let you all into the secret.

On a high shelf in a dark corner of a little-used library, there is a remarkable book. Bound in thick, dark leather that has become dry and cracked with age, the book is covered in a fine layer of dust. Brush aside the dust, and you will see, in ornate gold letters, the book's title.

If you were able to read the title (which you would *not* be, because it is in an ancient language that today is understood by only three people in the whole world) you would find yourself looking at the only known copy of *Wonderful Tales and Legends of the Land of Vàldovar, as Told to, and Here Recorded by, Vingetorix Popplehuff, Historian Royal to the Court of His Majesty King Ferdinand the Twentieth*.

Now, King Ferdinand the Twentieth's great interest was in the history of his country, and especially in the doings of his ancestors. These had all been colourful characters and all had made great contributions to Valdovarian culture. King Ferdinand the Third, for example, had introduced the Drumnovian Brown Pig into Vàldovar (and, according to some, also into the royal castle).

It was, however, one ancestor in particular who had always fascinated King Ferdinand the Twentieth, and that was his great-great-great-great-great-grandfather, King Ferdinand the Thirteenth, about whom many intriguing stories were still told around the firesides of Vàldovar. Ferdinand the Twentieth therefore commanded the learned historian, Vingetorix Popplehuff, to collect and record these stories.

It so happens that I am one of the three people who can still read the ancient language of Vàldovar, and so when, almost thirty years ago, I came across the copy of Popplehuff's book – which had clearly not been opened for at least a hundred years – you can well imagine my excitement.

I immediately set about translating the stories and retelling them for a modern readership. The first six stories appeared in *Magic in Vàldovar*. Now, in *Dreams of Vàldovar* you can read six more. I'm still polishing the translation of the last six (ancient Valdovarian is a fearsomely difficult language) and these will appear in due course in *Wonders of Vàldovar*.

As for the magnificent leather-bound copy of Popplehuff's original book – well, I returned it to its place on the high shelf in a dark corner of the little-used library and, as far as I know, there it remains to this day, gathering dust once more.

Neil Johnson, Over Kellet, 2006.

Dreaming of Vàldovar!

Beyond the restless, swelling sea,
Long years ago, and far away,
'Twixt mountains tall and forests dark,
A magic hidden land there lay.

Few now there are that know of it,
And fewer still to tell
Of things that happened in that land –
Though I remember well.

So once again, draw close to me,
And songs to you I'll sing
Of hills and vales of Vàldovar,
Of Wizard and of King.

Together we shall dream a dream
Of days of long ago,
And in that dream, I shall reveal
The wondrous things I know.

For I have talked with Princesses,
With unicorns and men,
With fiery-breathing dragon-kind,
And creatures living then,

That breathe not now – that into myth
Have passed, and there reside.
But I shall waken them again,
For you to walk beside.

And if, perchance, at story's end,
You feel yourself to be
In Vàldovar, that land afar,
With Lady of the Sea,

With Princess, Cook, and Conjuror,
Stonemason, Guardsman, King,
Then dreams have touched you from the songs
That I to you now sing.

A story is a dream, you see,
And dreams are stories, too.
And so, my little ones, I bring
My story-dreams to you.

The Princess

ong ago, in the far-off land of Vàldovar, there lived a wise King, whose name was Ferdinand the Thirteenth. King Ferdinand was a kind and gentle man. His favourite pastime was to walk out amongst his subjects and to spend the day talking to them; then he would stroll through the meadows, smelling the perfume of the small, blue Sky-petals that grew in rich profusion. He would next go to the leafy woods and watch the birds and the badgers and all the other small creatures that lived there. For King Ferdinand, *that* was the perfect day!

Queen Berenice, who was *very* beautiful, spent most of her mornings in the royal castle, where she made sure that the Servants and the Pageboys, the Ladies-in-waiting, the Guards and the Courtiers, all knew what their duties were and carried them out correctly.

When she was satisfied that everything was in order, Queen Berenice would call for her carriage, and she would go out of the castle and amongst the folk of Vàldovar. She would call upon the old and the sick, and anyone who needed help.

To some she would give food that she herself had made, and to others she would give blankets and warm clothing. In this way, Queen Berenice ensured that the people of Vàldovar were happy and contented.

King Ferdinand and Queen Berenice had a son, Prince Almeric. Almeric was a very happy young man, because he was shortly to be married to the Lady Britta. He was also very clever, because he knew lots of animal languages: he could speak to cats and dogs, rabbits and earwigs, cows and wupples (wupples are very strange, furry little animals found only in Vàldovar). Because of this, Almeric had many animal friends, and he was also able to use his special skills to help anyone in Vàldovar who had a problem with their pet.

So, you see, the people of Vàldovar had good reason to love their King, their Queen, and their Prince. They were the perfect Royal Family – or at least they *would* have been, if there had not been one problem: King Ferdinand and Queen Berenice had a daughter – the Princess Ianthe – and (to be perfectly honest) she was really *horrid*!

Ianthe was eight years old, and she was a pretty little girl. Unfortunately, she was also *very* badly behaved. She would speak rudely to the servants and say to them things like: 'Make my bed – and be quick about it!' or 'Hurry up, and bring me my hot milk – I want it *right now*.' She never said 'please' or 'thank you' or 'by your leave' or 'if you would not mind.' She never smiled at anyone, and she shouted all the time. If anything upset her, she would stamp her foot and throw her doll at the wall.

Once Ianthe tried to kick Mollinda, the Chambermaid, but she missed and fell on her back. This made her so angry that she ran around the castle, opening all the doors and banging them shut. She made such a noise that she gave everyone a terrible headache.

Nothing that Queen Berenice did seemed to have any effect on Ianthe. When the Queen scolded her, Ianthe sulked for two days and then pulled all the bedclothes off her bed and tied them all into such a big knot that it took four servants a whole day to untie it.

When the Queen promised to take Ianthe on a special trip to visit the Mountain Folk, if only Ianthe would be well-behaved, Ianthe replied: 'I don't want to go to see the silly Mountain Folk. All they talk about is hills and rocks and boring old things like that.' Then she ran to the window, flung it open, and shouted out: 'Silly old Mountain Folk, silly old Mountain Folk,' over and over again.

King Ferdinand knew nothing about his daughter's rudeness and temper tantrums. The servants, guardsmen, courtiers, and everyone else in the castle, did not say anything to him, and Queen Berenice did not want to bother her husband (a King has so many other things to worry about).

However, one day, King Ferdinand was walking down one of the long corridors in the castle when he heard Mollinda, the Chambermaid, singing. Mollinda was in one of the rooms, polishing and dusting, and, as she did so, she was singing a song that Theobaldus, the Court Musician, had composed. It went like this:

When Ianthe has a tantrum,
It's a dreadful thing to hear;
She bangs the door,
And stamps the floor,
And no-one dares go near.

She throws her dolly at the wall,
She kicks the chambermaid,
And tears her books.
Her nasty looks
Make everyone afraid.

Ianthe's really terrible –
A ghastly little mite.
One day, she cried:
'Don't try to hide.
I'll find you – then I'll bite!'

The servants in their quarters,
And the guardsmen in their tower,
Hate to see
Young Ianthe
Scowl horribly, and glower.

What can be done with Ianthe?
Oh, what will make her good?
If aught I knew
That I could do,
I'd do it – if I could!

King Ferdinand listened to the song, and then demanded to know why Mollinda was singing such terrible things about the Princess Ianthe. When Mollinda told him all about his daughter's bad behaviour, the King was astonished, and *very* upset, and he commanded that Ianthe should be brought before him in his throne room immediately.

'Now, my dear young lady,' he said sternly, as she stood before him. 'What is all this that I hear? I am told that you are rude to the servants, that you throw things at the walls, and that you bang all the castle doors when you want anything that you cannot have. Is this true?'

Ianthe shuffled her feet and scowled. 'I think all the servants are beastly,' she replied. 'After all, *I'm* a Princess, and everyone should do everything that I want.'

'My dear,' King Ferdinand replied, 'even though you are a Princess you must be polite and kind to everyone.'

'Well,' said Ianthe, stamping her foot, 'I'm *not* going to be nice. Being a Princess means that I *don't* have to be nice if I don't want to be. Anyway, I think *you* are even beastlier than the servants.'

All the Servants and Courtiers, the Guards and the Queen, gasped. No-one had ever before spoken to the King like that! It was quite unheard of.

King Ferdinand was extremely angry, but (because he was a very clever king) he did not let anyone see that his daughter's words had upset him. He said simply, 'Go to your chamber, Ianthe, and remain there until I say that you can come out. Your meals will be brought to you, and you will not speak to anyone – not to the servants, not to your brother, Prince Almeric, not to your mother, and most *certainly* not to me, until I have decided what must be done about your bad manners.'

At first, Ianthe refused to move, but King Ferdinand gave an order to Rufus, the Captain of the Guard. Captain Rufus was a very tall, and very strong man. He promptly picked up Princess Ianthe, tucked her under his arm and marched off with her. Although Ianthe struggled and squealed like a piglet, Captain Rufus was so big and strong that he did not notice. When he reached Ianthe's chamber, he opened the door, popped Ianthe inside, closed the door, and, taking a bunch of keys from his belt, locked it.

Ianthe was *furious*! However, no matter how hard she shouted, and no matter how many toys she threw at the walls, no-one took any notice. For the next five days, no-one spoke to Ianthe, and she took her meals in her room, all alone.

'Well,' said King Ferdinand to Queen Berenice on the sixth day, 'I think that Ianthe must have learned her lesson by now, and will be better-behaved.'

He was, however, quite wrong. When Ianthe was finally allowed out of her room, she first of all bit Mollinda the Chambermaid, then she kicked Old Joliphant the Butler, and then she just screamed and screamed at the top of her voice.

'You know, my dear,' said King Ferdinand to Queen Berenice, as they listened to the terrible noise that Ianthe was making, 'I think that there is only one thing left for me to do. I must go to seek the advice of the Wizard-who-lives-in-the-Wood.'

So the King ordered that his horse should be made ready and, when this was done, he set out on the journey to the Wood of Wishing.

He rode for two days and two nights until at last he reached the edge of the dark wood, where tangled Sharpthorn bushes and clumps of Strangleweed grew so densely that no-one could pass. Then the King called out:

Wood of Wishing, it is told
That thou art ruled by magic old.
Permit me to pass on my way,
When this – the Magic Word – I say.

After speaking these words, King Ferdinand said the magic word (only the Kings of Vàldovar, and very few others, know what the magic word is, and so I cannot tell it to you).

No sooner had the magic word passed the King's lips, than the tangled Sharpthorn bushes parted, and the clumps of Strangleweed and the trees and bushes swayed to one side, opening a path into the wood. Down this path the King rode, until, at last, he reached a clearing in the very centre of the wood.

The clearing was carpeted with fine, green grass and hundreds of tiny flowers of many different colours. In the middle of the clearing stood a mighty oak tree, as wide as a house. In the trunk of the oak was an enormous carved wooden door. King Ferdinand dismounted from his horse, strode up to the door, and smote upon it with his hand.

'Great Wizard,' he called. 'I wish to speak to you about an important matter.'

The great door, however, remained closed. Again, the

King banged upon it, this time using the hilt of his sword. Still there was no response. King Ferdinand thought for a moment and then he began to sing a little song.

Sing hey for the Wizard,
Sing hey for his tree;
Come, ancient Wizard,
Come speak with me.
Open now your oaken door,
And tread the flowered forest floor.

My tale I'll tell,
Then thou thy spell
Shall quickly cast,
So that, at last,
All shall be well
In Vàldovar.

Sing ho for the Wizard,
Sing ho for his tree;
Come, ancient Wizard,
Come talk with me.
I smite upon your oaken door,
And seek your magic help once more.

Suddenly, with a creaking of ancient hinges, the heavy wooden door began to open, and, from the darkness within, emerged the Wizard-who-lives-in-the-Wood. He wore a long, blue cloak, embroidered with silver stars, and a tall, white, pointed hat, decorated with blue moons. In his hand he carried a stout wooden staff which he pointed at King Ferdinand.

'What was that dreadful noise?' demanded the Wizard.

'I was singing,' said King Ferdinand.

'*Singing?*' the Wizard replied, raising his thick, bushy, white eyebrows in astonishment. 'Is that what you call it? I thought there must be at least five cats having a fight. Well, no matter. Now that I have been wakened from my slumber, I must enquire what brings you, King Ferdinand the Thirteenth, once again to the Wood of Wishing.'

King Ferdinand explained to the Wizard just how badly behaved Princess Ianthe was, and how nothing that anyone could do seemed to have the slightest effect in improving her manners.

The Wizard listened in silence, and then he thought hard, stroking his long, white beard as he did so.

After some moments, he smiled and said: 'I know exactly what we have to do. Listen carefully, and then go from this place and follow my instructions precisely.'

From the folds of his robe, the Wizard drew a small leather pouch which he handed to King Ferdinand.

'In this pouch,' said the Wizard, 'are four pearls. The first of these is of purest white, the second of deepest black, the third of brightest red, and the fourth (which is the rarest of all pearls) of gleaming gold.'

King Ferdinand took the pouch and asked: 'But how will these pearls help to improve the behaviour of my daughter, the Princess Ianthe?'

'Patience, King Ferdinand,' the Wizard replied. 'Pray allow me to continue. You must take them to Mellindorf the Toymaker, and command him to make four things.

'The first is to be a doll fashioned in the exact likeness of the Princess Ianthe, with the white pearl, threaded on fine silk, hanging around her neck.

'The second is to take the form of a dog, with the black pearl being used to create one of its eyes.

'The third is to be a spinning-top onto which is to be set the red pearl.

'The final pearl – the pearl of shining gold – is to be set into a silver crown that fits perfectly the Princess Ianthe.

'When these four things have been made, Mellindorf is to take them at midnight to the foot of the great and ancient yew tree that grows near to his workshop. There, in the light of the moon, he is to sing this song.' The Wizard then told King Ferdinand the words of a magic song that Mellindorf was required to sing.

King Ferdinand scratched his head (which is actually a bit difficult when you are wearing a crown). 'I really cannot see how giving Ianthe presents will stop her being so naughty,' he said.

'Well,' replied the Wizard, 'if you were a Wizard you would understand. But you are not, and that is why you don't. So go, King Ferdinand the Thirteenth, and do as I say, and you shall see for yourself the magic of the pearls.'

King Ferdinand rode away from the Wood of Wishing to the small village where Mellindorf the Toymaker had his workshop. Mellindorf was an old man who wore a bright red cloak trimmed with white ermine. He had a bushy white beard and white eyebrows that stuck right out.

'Welcome, King Ferdinand,' said Mellindorf. 'It is many years since I last had the honour to greet you in my workshop. Tell me how I may now be of service to you.'

King Ferdinand showed Mellindorf the four pearls that he had received from the Wizard. He then explained how the white pearl was to hang around the neck of a doll fashioned in the likeness of the Princess Ianthe; how the black pearl was to form one eye of a toy dog; how the red pearl was to be set into a spinning-top; and how the shining golden pearl was to grace a silver crown that would fit the Princess Ianthe. King Ferdinand then told Mellindorf of the song that had to be sung when the toys had been made.

Mellindorf bowed. 'Everything shall be done as you say, your Majesty,' he said.

'And with haste, too, I trust,' said the King.

'In four days' time I shall come to your castle,' replied Mellindorf, 'and I shall bring with me the toys and the silver crown, over which the Wizard's spell has been cast.'

So King Ferdinand left the four pearls with Mellindorf and returned to his castle.

Mellindorf was as good as his word. He made the toys exactly as the Wizard had instructed, and took them at midnight to the great and ancient yew tree that stood close to his workshop. There he sang the Wizard's song:

O, toys that under midnight sky,
These precious pearls display,
Receive this magic where you lie,
And hear what I now say.

White pearl,
Black pearl,
Red pearl,
Gold:
Waken now thy magic old,
And with Ianthe thus be bold.

Black pearl,
Red pearl,
Gold pearl,
White:
Magic given on this night
Shall teach Ianthe what is right.

Red pearl,
Gold pearl,
White pearl,
Black:
Nought of magic shalt thou lack.
To sweetness draw Ianthe back.

Gold pearl,
White pearl,
Black pearl,
Red:
The magic spell has now been said.
Ianthe shall to love be led.

Each toy that under silver moon
Bears thus its magic pearl,
Shall change the naughty child into
A kindly little girl.

Four days later, Mellindorf arrived at the castle with four boxes, each gaily wrapped in brightly coloured paper and tied with silver ribbons. On each parcel was a label which read:

The Princess Ianthe

The Royal Castle

Vàldovar

Mellindorf was shown into the great hall where King Ferdinand and Queen Berenice sat upon their golden thrones. Princess Ianthe was sitting on a stool, tearing up sheets of paper and throwing pieces all over the floor. As fast as the servants rushed to tidy it all up, she tore up more paper and tossed it into the air.

When Ianthe saw the labels on the parcels that Mellindorf carried, she squealed: 'Those are for *me*!' Then she rushed from her stool and seized the four parcels.

'Ianthe!' Queen Berenice said sternly. 'You should not take things without asking permission politely, and most certainly not without saying "thank you" afterwards. Now, please apologize to Mellindorf the Toymaker for the rudeness that you have shown to him.'

'No, I won't!' cried Ianthe. 'The parcels are mine. I want them.' Then, clutching the parcels, she ran from the great hall, up the twisty stairs, to her bedroom. There she started to tear open the parcels, pulling off the silver ribbons and flinging the coloured wrapping paper all over the floor.

The first parcel that she opened contained the doll with the silver pearl necklace.

'Oh,' exclaimed Ianthe, 'she's just like me!'

Then she opened the second parcel and took out the little white toy dog with the black pearl eye.

'Ugh!' said Ianthe. 'I don't like this. One of its eyes is blue and the other is black. What a *silly* toymaker Mellindorf is.'

Then she opened the third parcel. In it she found the spinning-top in which was set the red pearl.

'I can leave this lying on the floor of my bedroom,' said Ianthe, 'then one of the servants is sure to trip on it and fall over.' (You see how horrid Ianthe really was!)

When she tried to open the last parcel (which, you remember, contained the golden pearl set into a silver crown) the ribbon refused to come off, and, try as she might, Ianthe could not tear the wrapping paper. Angrily, she flung the parcel into a far corner of the room.

'I don't care *what* is inside,' she said. 'It is probably a really *nasty* toy.'

She turned to the the princess doll, the dog, and the spinning-top, and placed them all in a row and looked at them.

'I wonder who sent me these presents?' she thought.

'Anyway, I don't care. I'm a Princess, and I *should* get lots of presents all the time.'

Suddenly, a very strange thing happened. The princess doll with the white pearl necklace came alive and ran about the room, waving her arms in the air, and squealing at the top of her voice! Ianthe was so surprised that she fell over. The princess doll was making such a dreadful noise, that Ianthe's ears started to hurt.

'Stop it,' she shouted. 'Stop making that awful noise *this instant.*'

But the princess doll took no notice at all. She ran round and round the room, faster and faster, and shouting and squealing even harder.

Then, without any warning, the toy dog with the black pearl eye also came alive. It started to bark and bark, and yap and yap, and it too ran around Ianthe's bedroom, biting the furniture and tearing at the carpet with its sharp little teeth.

'You horrid dog!' cried Ianthe. 'Come here at once and be quiet.'

The dog rushed at Ianthe and started biting her shoes, and Ianthe had to jump onto her bed to escape.

All at once there was a whirring and a whining noise, and the spinning-top started to spin. Faster and faster it spun – the red pearl that was set into it winking and flashing. The spinning-top whirled around the room, crashing into chairs and sending them tumbling across the floor.

Ianthe clapped her hands over her ears, but it was no use. She could not shut out the shouting and squealing of the princess doll, the barking and yapping of the toy dog, and the whirring and whining of the spinning-top. Her head was starting to ache. Her lovely bedroom was being ruined. Broken chairs lay everywhere, and the carpets, bedclothes and curtains were in shreds and tatters.

'You naughty, *naughty* toys,' wailed Ianthe. 'I *do* wish you would be good.'

As soon as she said these words, the princess doll stopped running about and squealing, the toy dog stopped barking, and the spinning-top stopped spinning.

'Well,' said the princess doll to Ianthe, 'why *should* we be good? *You* are never good, are you?'

Then the toys started running and yapping and spinning all over again, making even more noise than before.

'Oh, do please stop!' cried Princess Ianthe. 'Please be good. If you will be good, I … I … *promise* that I shall be good, too.'

In the spinning top, the red pearl suddenly glowed even more brightly than before; the toy dog looked at Ianthe with its black pearl eye; and the princess doll said: 'Do you *really* promise, Ianthe?'

'Oh yes,' said Ianthe, 'really, I do. Just please stop making all that noise, and do stop tearing and breaking everything in my bedroom.'

As soon as she said these words, the princess doll, the toy dog, and the spinning-top, all became still and turned back into ordinary toys once again.

Then Ianthe picked up the parcel that she had not been able to open (she did not know that this was the one that contained the silver crown with the golden pearl) and returned to the great hall where her father, King Ferdinand, and her mother, Queen Berenice, sat on their golden thrones. Ianthe went up to them, hung her head, and said: 'I am sorry I have been so horrid. I promise that in future I shall always be *really* good and well-behaved.'

The King was so surprised that his crown fell off, and the Queen was so surprised that she dropped the book she was reading.

'Well,' said King Ferdinand, 'I am delighted to hear you say so, my dear,' and he held out his hand to Ianthe, and bade her sit beside him on his golden throne.

At that moment, the parcel that Ianthe was carrying suddenly jumped out of her arms and onto the floor. The silver ribbon untied itself. The gaily coloured wrapping paper fell away. The box opened, and out floated the beautiful silver crown that Mellindorf the Toymaker had made. In the crown was set the pearl of gleaming gold.

King Ferdinand, Queen Berenice and Princess Ianthe watched in amazement as the silver crown floated up and up and up, and settled gently upon Princess Ianthe's head. Then, from the crown, came a soft, musical voice, singing:

Oh, a crown of gold
(Or so I'm told)
Suits a haughty, royal King-o,
And his regal Queen
(For this I've seen)
Wears a shiny golden ring-o.

Oh, a crown of zinc
(Or so I think)
To a Pageboy's quite becoming,
But a crown of lead
(On a Prince's head)
I think would be quite numbing.

Now, a crown of brass
(Oh, alack, alas)
Much polishing requires,
And a crown of steel
(I rather feel)
No handsome Earl desires.

Oh, a wooden crown
(It makes me frown!)
Would appear so very silly,
While a crown of string
(Is there such a thing?),
Would dangle willy-nilly.

Oh, a crown I be
(Just look at me)
Of the finest silver moulded,
And my golden pearl
(Oh, little girl)
Means you'll no more be scolded.

So you be good
(You said you would)
And I'll adorn your tresses,
For a silver crown
(Of great renown)
Is essential for Princesses.

Princess Ianthe laughed and clapped her hands, and said to King Ferdinand: 'Does this mean that if I am very, *very* good, and not ever naughty, I can wear this beautiful silver crown?'

'Of course, my dear,' the King replied with a smile. '*Only* Princesses who are always kind and considerate to other people can wear a silver crown bearing a golden pearl. This is well known.'

And so it was that the Princess Ianthe became a good little Princess, and she was so helpful and polite that soon everyone in Vàldovar came to love her as much as they loved King Ferdinand, Queen Berenice, Prince Almeric and the Lady Britta.

But, of course, she was still only a little girl, and sometimes (but only *very* occasionally) she would be tempted to be just a teeny-weeny bit naughty (I am sure that you know how difficult it is to be good *all* the time). Whenever this happened, Ianthe went up to her bedroom and there the toy dog with the black pearl eye would bark softly, the spinning-top with the red pearl set into it would spin gently with a low whirring sound, and the princess doll with the white pearl necklace would open her eyes, wag her finger, and say 'Do be careful, Princess Ianthe. Remember that only very kind and polite little Princesses may wear a silver crown.'

And Ianthe would think for a little while, and then she would smile and promise, once again, to be good.

Back in the Wood of Wishing, a song-thrush flew down into the clearing in the very centre of the wood, and alighted upon the shoulder of the Wizard-who-lives-in-the-Wood. The thrush trilled into the Wizard's ear a pretty song that told of how the magic pearls had brought Mellindorf's wonderful toys to life, and how the Princess Ianthe had finally understood how horrid it was when people were naughty, unkind and impolite. Then the thrush told how Ianthe had received her silver crown.

The Wizard smiled and said: 'I am delighted that Ianthe is now so well-behaved, kind, polite, and courteous. She is, indeed, a *true* Princess!'

Still trilling its sweet music, the song-thrush flew up into the trees, up, up, and into the clear blue sky.

And, still smiling, the Wizard-who-lives-in-the-Wood went back into his home in the ancient oak tree. Behind him, the great carved door swung shut.

The Sea Lady

The tiny realm of Vàldovar
From other lands lies hidden,
And few there are that from afar
Come to its fields unbidden.

For west and east proud mountains stand;
Great forests to the north lie;
Swells southerly the foamy sea
O'er which the calling gulls fly.

The roaring waves, the silent deeps,
The swelling tide that reaches
Like grasping hand toward the land
And Vàldovar's broad beaches,

Are feared by most – though not by all –
And there begins my story.
I sing to thee of storm-flecked sea,
And she who loved its glory.

o well hidden is the little country of Vàldovar, that very few people know that it even exists. It is tucked away between two ranges of high, snow-covered mountains. Where the mountains end, deep, deep forests begin. A stormy sea guards Vàldovar's shore.

Most of the people live in Vàldovar's pretty villages which lie amongst that country's gentle hills and flower-filled meadows. Hardly any of the Valdovarians ever go near the sea, being rather frightened by the enormous waves that crash upon the shore.

However, I want to tell you the story of a maiden who did *not* fear the sea. Her name was Marinella (which, in the ancient language of Vàldovar, means *she who loves the sea*). Even when she was a little child, Marinella spent most of her time running along the golden beach, laughing when the salty sea-spray blew into her face, and shouting with delight whenever she saw, far out to sea, a dolphin or mighty swordfish leaping and sporting amongst the waves.

'Oh do take care, Marinella,' her parents would say. 'Do not go too near the sea. A great wave might fall upon you and carry you out, far from the shore.' But Marinella did not heed them – and one day, that is *exactly* what happened.

The day was bright, but very windy. Little clouds scurried across the blue sky, and the haunting calls of the soaring, diving gulls were lost amongst the roar and clamour of the wild, wild sea. Marinella gazed in wonder as wave after giant wave rose and fell. So fascinated was she, that she drew closer and closer to the sea, giggling as her bare feet were tickled by bubbles and her toes sank into the wet sand.

All at once, there was a noise like thunder. Marinella looked up and there, rushing towards her, was a giant wave – an enormous wall of green water that towered above her head. Marinella squealed and turned to run away. Too late! The wave fell upon her. She was swept from her feet, and she felt herself being borne away as the wave died and drew back into the sea.

Down, down, into the depths Marinella sank. At first, she could see nothing but green water and millions of swirling bubbles. Suddenly, a large, grey shape floated into view. It was a beautiful dolphin. The dolphin looked at Marinella with its soft, gentle eyes and then, with a flick of its tail, it swept her onto its back and began to swim upwards, towards the surface of the sea. At last, the dolphin leapt out of the water, with Marinella holding on tightly to its fin.

The dolphin bore Marinella back to the shore. As she stepped once again onto the sand, she turned and thanked the dolphin for having saved her. The dolphin whistled and squeaked. If Prince Almeric had been there he would have been able to tell Marinella what the dolphin had said (because, as you know, Prince Almeric can speak the languages of many animals).

In fact, the dolphin had replied: 'I am very happy to have helped you, my dear young lady. I and my brother and sister dolphins have often seen you as you walk on the shore, and we know how much you love the sea.'

Then the dolphin turned and raced back out to sea, and Marinella watched him as he leapt gracefully from wave to wave until at last he disappeared over the horizon.

When Marinella told her parents what had happened, they were greatly alarmed. 'We warned you, Marinella, that it could be dangerous for you to go too near to the sea,' they said, and Marinella promised to be more careful in future.

'Remember, Marinella,' said her father, 'that there may not be a dolphin to save you if you are swept into the sea again.'

As the years passed, Marinella grew to be a beautiful maiden. One day, as she was walking on the sea shore, she saw a shape lying on the sand, at the water's edge. Drawing closer, she realized that it was a young man, dressed in the clothes of a sailor. Quickly, she ran to him and, kneeling down on the wet sand, raised his head in her hands. As she did so, he opened his eyes.

'Oh,' he gasped, 'where am I?'

'This is Vàldovar,' Marinella replied. 'How did you come to be here, lying on the shore?'

'We were shipwrecked,' said the sailor. 'Our ship struck a great rock and sank. My comrades swam to an island and were saved, but I sank beneath the waves. Then a dolphin came and took me upon its back and brought me here to this shore.'

Marinella wondered whether the dolphin that had saved the sailor was the same one that, years before, had saved her. *I think it was. What do you think?*

She helped the young man to his feet, and together they walked back to her parents' cottage.

'What am I to do?' said the sailor. 'I have no ship to which I can return, and no-one knows that I am here in Vàldovar.'

'We shall be very pleased to have you stay here with us, if you wish,' said Marinella's mother. 'You can help my husband with the work on our small farm.'

The sailor was delighted to do so. Marinella was also very pleased, because she thought that the sailor was really very handsome. And so it was that the sailor, whose name was Petrosian, came to live in the land of Vàldovar. He had a cheery manner and a ready smile, and he and Marinella spent many hours together, walking the green hills and wooded valleys, and strolling on the golden beaches of Vàldovar. Over the following days and weeks, Marinella and Petrosian grew to love each other, and one year later they were married.

Athelstar, the Songwriter, composed a little song, which he sang at their wedding. It was a strange song, and the words at the end puzzled everyone, but the tune was lovely and Athelstar sang in a soft, deep voice.

Happy, happy Marinella
(She who loves the sea),
Whom gentle, caring dolphin saved,
Sing I this song to thee.
Petrosian, a sailor bold,
By dolphin borne to land
From shipwreck on the stormy sea
Today will take thine hand.
The angry waters, green and deep,
That once swept both away,
Were by a dolphin conquerèd,
And, on this joyous day,
Petrosian a promise makes
To thee, his wedded wife,
That by the shore, for ever more,
Shall be your married life.
By day the sound of swirling surf,
By night the tumbling wave,
Shall be your music, and recall
How dolphin, kind and brave,
Brought him to thee, saved thee for him,
And may, perchance, one day,
Come once again, his aid to bring
(This is the dolphin's way.)

As Athelstar the Songwriter had foretold, Petrosian built a small cottage close to the shore, and there he and Marinella lived happily. Every day they would go onto the sand, walk down to the water's edge, and gather the brightly-coloured shells and shiny pebbles that lay there in abundance. Taking these back to their cottage, they fashioned them into wonderful necklaces and brooches, which they then sold in the village markets of Vàldovar. The people of Vàldovar thought that the things that Marinella and her husband made were wonderful. They would come from the farthest parts of the land to purchase them, for they made excellent gifts for birthdays or weddings.

Although Marinella and Petrosian were contented with their life by the sea, Marinella sometimes noticed her husband gazing out over the tumbling waves, with a look of longing in his eyes. She understood what he was thinking.

'Dear Petrosian,' she said to him one day, 'why do you not build a small boat, so that you may again sail upon the sea?'

Petrosian smiled. 'Yes,' he said, 'I should like once more to feel the swell of the sea and the hand of the wind against the sail.'

The very next day, Petrosian started to build his boat, and Marinella helped him. Within a few weeks, it was was ready. The boat was just big enough to carry the two of them. Painted a gay yellow, and bearing a smart white sail on which Marinella had embroidered a leaping dolphin, the little boat bobbed merrily on the waves.

'Come,' said Petrosian, holding out his hand to Marinella, 'let us sail our little boat upon the sea.'

Although Marinella had never been in a boat before, she was not afraid, and she joined Petrosian in the boat. Together they spent the rest of the day sailing off the shore of Vàldovar.

Thereafter, Petrosian and Marinella would sail together every day. One day, however, Marinella said to her husband: 'I must go to take some necklaces and brooches to the markets of Vàldovar. Will you come with me?'

Petrosian, however, replied that he wished to sail their little boat to a beach where he had noticed some handsome pink and yellow shells.

'We could put such shells into the special necklaces that we are going to make for the Feast of Flowers,' he said.

Marinella agreed. She gathered together all the pretty things that she was to take to market, and then waved to her husband as he sailed away.

Suddenly, the sky grew very dark and a great wind rose up. The sea, that had been calm, began to heave and churn. The storm wind caught the sail of the little boat and Marinella could only watch helplessly as Petrosian and the boat were borne away, far from shore. Eventually, they were so far away that Marinella could no longer see them.

She put away the necklaces and brooches and sat down on a rock. 'Petrosian, my dear husband, knows the ways of the sea,' she thought. 'For many years he was a sailor and travelled, in fine weather and in storm, to many different lands. He will surely be able to sail our little boat safely back to the shore of Vàldovar.'

But though she waited all day, Petrosian did not return. When night came, Marinella returned to their cottage and lit a small candle which she placed in a window looking out on the sea. 'Petrosian will see this light,' she said to herself, 'and it will guide him back to me.'

The next day, Marinella again went down to the shore and sat on the rock, and waited, but still Petrosian did not return. The next day, and the next, Marinella waited. And so it went. Day after day, Marinella took her place on the rock and hoped and hoped for the return of her husband – but in vain.

The days, the weeks, the months, and then the years passed. Marinella no longer gathered the gaily coloured shells, no longer made the necklaces and brooches that the people of Vàldovar so loved, no longer smiled. She ate little, and her beauty faded. Every night she lit the little candle in the window of her cottage; every day she spent sitting on her rock on the shore and gazing out over the sea. The people of Vàldovar were very sad for Marinella. Gradually, they stopped calling her by her name, and referred to her simply as the *Sea Lady*.

One morning, Aramand the Shepherd, who was tending his flock in the meadow that runs right down to the shore, noticed that Marinella had not emerged from her cottage. She had not gone down to the shore, and was not sitting upon the rock, as she had done every day for so many years. Aramand went quickly to her cottage and knocked upon the door. When there was no answer, he pushed the door open and looked inside. Marinella was lying on her bed; her eyes were closed and she seemed hardly to be breathing.

Aramand ran quickly to the nearest village where Doctor Abladur, the Physician, lived. When Doctor Abladur and the other villagers heard what Aramand had to say, they all hurried to Marinella's cottage. Doctor Abladur went inside and, after a few minutes, came out again.

'I think, dear friends,' he said, 'that the Sea Lady is fading. Her heart has been broken by the loss, so many years ago, of Petrosian, her husband.'

'There must be *something* that can be done,' cried Cristolf the Baker.

Doctor Abladur shook his head. 'There is no medicine that I possess, nor any of which I know, that can cure her.'

'Then,' said Utherion the Artist, 'we must speak to the King, and seek his help.'

The people of Vàldovar loved their king, King Ferdinand the Thirteenth, and they knew that he would help them if he could. So they returned to the castle where King Ferdinand and Queen Berenice lived.

Like everyone else in Vàldovar, King Ferdinand knew of the Sea Lady and the story of how she had first found and then lost her husband.

'This is sad news, indeed,' he said, when he was told how the Sea Lady lay fading in her cottage by the sea. 'I do not know, however, what I can do, when even the good Doctor Abladur can find nothing in his art to save her.'

King Ferdinand thought for a moment, and then he said: 'I shall go to seek wisdom from the Wizard-who-lives-in-the-Wood.'

He commanded that his finest horse be prepared immediately and, when this was done, he mounted and rode for two days and two nights. He came at last to the Wood of Wishing, but the trees grew so closely together that his path was barred, and nowhere could he find a way by which he could enter the wood.

King Ferdinand then called, in a clear voice:

Wood of Wishing, harken well.
Thine ancient trees, 'neath ancient spell,
That bar my path, apart must stand.
Make way for your King Ferdinand!

He then spoke the magic word that is known only to the Kings of Vàldovar and to few others. As he did so, the trees before him moved slowly apart, revealing an ancient path leading to the middle of the wood. King Ferdinand rode his horse down this path until he reached a clearing where stood a mighty oak tree. In the oak was a huge door, upon which King Ferdinand banged with the hilt of his sword.

Slowly, the great door opened, and from the depths of the tree emerged the Wizard-who-lives-in-the-Wood. He wore a blue cloak on which twinkled many silver stars, and on his head was a long, pointed white hat decorated with blue moons.

'So, King Ferdinand the Thirteenth,' boomed the Wizard, 'you have yet again used the magic word to gain entry to my wood! My trees are old and wish to live in peace. They do not like to have to move aside to let a stranger pass.'

'*I* am no stranger,' replied King Ferdinand. 'I remind you, Great Wizard, that I am King of the land wherein lies this wood. The magic word is mine to use when I have need of your service.'

'Well said!' the Wizard laughed. 'So speak, King Ferdinand, and tell me what problem brings you now to the Wood of Wishing.'

King Ferdinand then told the Wizard of how Marinella, the Sea Lady, lay in her cottage by the sea, and how she was fading of a broken heart.

'I know well this sorrowful tale,' said the Wizard. 'Delphis the Dolphin told Aark the Albatross, and Aark the Albatross told me, of how a sudden storm drove the boat of Petrosian out across the sea, away from his wife. I know, too, of the vigil that she has kept these many years, sitting on a lonely rock on the shore.'

The Wizard closed his eyes and thought for a moment. Then he said: 'This is what you must do, King Ferdinand – and do it quickly. Seek Athelstar the Songwriter. Bid him go down to the shore, and there to sing a song to the sea.'

'A song to the sea!' said King Ferdinand, in surprise. 'How will singing a song remove this sadness from the Sea Lady?'

The Wizard smiled. 'The power of music is greater than you know, dear King,' he replied. 'Go. Do as I have said, and you shall see.'

So King Ferdinand returned to his Castle, summoned Athelstar the Songwriter, and told him what the Wizard had said. Athelstar bowed. 'It shall be done, my Lord,' he said, and, with no more ado, he, King Ferdinand, Doctor Abladur, and a great crowd of Valdovarians, went down to the shore.

By now, night had fallen, but the sea and the shore were bathed in the silver light of a full moon. Marinella's cottage, though, lay dark and silent, and the candle that she had lit every night for so many years, no longer flickered in the window. Athelstar faced the sea, and began to sing.

I sing you my song of the shimmering sea,
Of fishes and dolphins, and creatures that be
In the emerald depths where the water is cool,
And the clear, sparkling world of the rocky shore pool;
Of Dogfish and Catfish, of Mullet and Crab,
Of tentacled Octopus, Herring and Dab,
And Starfish, Anemones, Urchins that creep,
And the bright open waters where Porpoises leap.

I sing of the Marlin, the Whiting and Cod,
The Plaice in the net, and the Fluke on the rod,
The Tuna and Gurnard – and now I'll relate
How the Haddock and Pilchard, and Salmon and Skate,
Love the water that's light – not the water that's dark
(For there lurk the Squid and the sinister Shark).
To silvery sea-bed the Lobster is drawn,
To sport with the Crayfish, the Shrimp and the Prawn.

I sing of the Limpet and Barnacle black,
Of Rocks where they cling, and of Coral and Wrack.
In beds where the Sea-grass its dark fronds unfurls,
The wrinkle-shelled Oysters lie guarding their pearls.
Of Scallops and Ormers my story-song tells,
Of Cockles and Mussels, and Clams in their shells.
In the silent abyss, where the Angler-fish feel
Their way in the dark, lives the sinuous Eel.

I sing of the Jellyfish, Monkfish and Trout,
Of the Swordfish and Mackerel – and do not doubt
That the Sole, Hake, and Halibut, Garfish and Ray,
'Neath swell of the wave, weave their watery way
Past Seahorse and Sponge, through the Plankton and Krill.
In a wreck on the seabed the Moray lies still;
Whilst riding the wave that is lashed by the gale
Is the King of the Sea – the magnificent Whale!

My song is now over – my song of the sea.
I call on you creatures, wherever you be,
In the pools of the shore, in the wave, in the deep,
To help the Sea Lady her courage to keep.
Come Dolphin, come Whale, and come Seagull, come Fish.
Oh, come to her, come to her. Grant her one wish.
That now and forever, rejoinèd she'll be
With her storm-stolen loved one, long lost to the sea.

No sooner had Athelstar ended his song, than a very strange thing happened. The sea began to churn and foam as hundreds of sea-creatures came to the surface and made their way to the shore. They came out of the water and onto the beach and slowly, slowly, made their way towards the cottage where Marinella lay.

Through the doorway and into the cottage they poured,

and King Ferdinand and all the others who had gathered on the shore, heard, from inside the cottage, a sound like the gentle lapping of waves, and the calling of seagulls, the singing of whales and dolphins, and the soft bubbling that comes from the mouths of fishes.

Then, from the doorway, there emerged a dolphin (and I really think that it was the *very same* dolphin that had rescued Marinella from the sea when she was a child, and that had brought Petrosian safely to land when he had been shipwrecked). The people who were watching, gasped. For there, riding on the back of the dolphin, was Marinella!

As the dolphin moved slowly down towards the sea, followed by all the other sea-creatures, it could be seen that a wonderful change had come over Marinella. She was once again young and beautiful, and her thin, grey hair was now long, dark and shining. But the most extraordinary thing was that her legs had become transformed into a wonderful, shiny tail, like that of a fish, all covered in golden scales.

When the dolphin reached the sea, Marinella slid quickly from its back, and, with a swish of her tail, began to swim out into the moonlit waves.

Suddenly, all the people started to cheer and wave their arms in the air. For there, swimming towards the Sea Lady, was *another* figure. It was Petrosian! And he, like Marinella, was young and strong. As they met, they leapt with cries of joy from the water into the air, and all could see that *both* bore wonderful, golden fish tails. Marinella and Petrosian turned and waved to King Ferdinand and his subjects, and then, hand in hand, began to swim out into the open sea.

There are some who say that, at night, when the moon is full and the air is calm, Marinella and Petrosian may be seen, sitting together on a rock, some way out into the sea. Marinella combs her long, dark, shining hair. Petrosian sings softly to her, and she to him.

Petrosian

Thy sailor is returnèd home,
Returnèd from the sea.
No more the waters shall I roam,
I am come back to thee.
Ah! The sea.
Ah! The sea.
I am come back to thee.

Marinella

I swim, I swim to thee, my love,
Through gentle moonlit wave,
To bring to thee my heart, my love,
My soul for thee to save.
Ah! The wave.
Ah! The wave.
My soul for thee to save.

Petrosian

Swim thou again to me, my love,
Through clear and crystal wave,
And bring to me thy heart, my love,
Thy soul I vow to save
Ah! The wave.
Ah! The wave.
Thy soul I vow to save.

Marinella

Thou com'st again to me, my love,
Through waters cold and deep,
To claim me as thine own, my love,
My love for e'er to keep.
Ah! The deep.
Ah! The deep.
My love for e'er to keep.

Petrosian

Ah, yes, I come to thee, my love,
Across the oceans deep,
And claim thee as mine own, my love,
Thy love for e'er to keep.
Ah! The deep.
Ah! The deep.
Thy love for e'er to keep.

Marinella and Petrosian

We both are now returnèd home
Returnèd to the sea,
No more to wait, no more to roam –
Together shall we be
(Ah! The sea.
Ah! The sea.)
For all eternity!

There are others who say that, around the rock on which Marinella and Petrosian sit, a large, grey dolphin swims, and, from time to time, leaps joyously from the sea.

Back in the Wood of Wishing, Aark the Albatross flew down into the clearing where stood the Wizard-who-lives-in-the-Wood.

'What news, old friend?' asked the Wizard, and Aark told him how the sea creatures had used the Magic of the Deep to fulfil the Sea Lady's wish. The Wizard smiled. 'I am happy for the Lady and for her husband,' he said. Then he sighed. 'But I am tired. Making magic is weary work!'

And the Wizard-who-lives-in-the-Wood went back into his home in the ancient oak. Behind him, the great carved door swung shut.

The Captain of the Guard

I n the royal castle of King Ferdinand the Thirteenth of Vàldovar, the Captain of the Guard was a man called Rufus. You may remember that it was Captain Rufus who had once tucked Princess Ianthe under his arm and carried her, kicking and squealing, up to her bedroom, after she had been very, *very* impertinent to her father, King Ferdinand.

Well, I am now going to tell you a story about Captain Rufus, and how he was called upon to catch a thief. First, however, let me tell you a little about Captain Rufus himself.

He was a very fine figure of a man. He was tall, with broad shoulders, and he walked with his head held high and his back straight – as, of course, every good soldier should.

He wore a splendid blue uniform with lots of gold braid all over it, and a three-cornered hat which had a large, fluffy feather on one side. His boots were black and *always* very shiny.

What everyone noticed most about Captain Rufus, however, was his fine moustache, which stuck out sideways and curled up at the ends. Captain Rufus was very proud of his moustache. 'A Captain without a moustache,' he would say, 'is like an egg-and-spoon race without a spoon – not *natural*!'

Every morning, Captain Rufus got up just before the sun rose. First, he inspected the castle guards, to see they were all smart; and then he went out, across the drawbridge, to where the King's band was waiting in front of the royal castle. With Captain Rufus at its head, the band marched right around the outside of the castle three times, with drums banging, fifes piping, and trumpets calling, to make quite sure that everyone inside the castle was wide awake and ready to start the day.

King Ferdinand was not quite sure that this was a good idea. 'After all,' he said, '*I* am the King, and *I* – and *not* Captain Rufus – should decide when I get up each morning.' But the military band had been doing its morning wake-up ceremony for as long as anyone could remember, and King Ferdinand never liked to interfere with tradition.

And anyway, King Ferdinand and Queen Berenice knew how much the Captain of the Guard loved the music of his band, because they had heard him one day singing, in his deep military voice:

I rise at dawn 'most every morn
(A soldier's life is hard).
I'm fit and spry, and that is why
I'm the Captain of the Guard.

Pom tiddly om
Tiddly om pom pom.
Pom tiddly om pom –
*Pom **pom**.*

Since once a boy, the greatest joy
I found in all the land,
Was marching to the great to-do
Of a military band.

Oh, Pom tiddly om
Tiddly om pom pom.
Pom tiddly om pom –
*Pom **pom**.*

I say to you (and this is true)
There's nothing quite so grand,
When you are sad (and the news is bad),
As a military band.

Oh, Pom tiddly om
Tiddly om pom pom.
Pom tiddly om pom –
*Pom **pom**.*

Ah, the thrill of the drum (tarum, tarum),
With the wailing of the fife,
And the trumpet clear – did you ever hear
Such a sound in all your life?

Oh, Pom tiddly om
Tiddly om pom pom.
Pom tiddly om pom –
*Pom **pom**.*

By the King and Queen, I've always been
Held in most high regard.
That's why, you see, I'll always be
The Captain of the Guard!

Yes, Pom tiddly om
Tiddly om pom pom.
Pom tiddly om pom –
*Pom **pom**!*

Captain Rufus was very proud of the way he and his company of guards looked after the King and Queen and all the many others who lived in the royal castle. Every evening he would make sure that all the castle doors were locked so that no thief could creep in and steal anything.

He was therefore *very* upset when, one morning, Mollinda and Bellinda, the two Chambermaids, came to him and Bellinda said: 'Oh, Captain Rufus, please come quickly. Mollinda has had a pretty ring stolen from her bedchamber.'

'Impossible!' said Captain Rufus. 'I remember shutting and locking all the castle doors last night when everyone had gone to bed. *No-one* could have entered the castle.'

Nevertheless, he accompanied them both to Mollinda's bedchamber, and there Mollinda showed him the tray on her dressing table where, each night before retiring, she would place the ring from her finger, together with the necklace that, many years ago, had been made by Marinella and Petrosian using small, shiny, coloured stones from the beaches of Vàldovar. The necklace was still there on the tray; the ring, however, was not.

'It was such a *lovely* ring,' said Mollinda, sadly. 'It was made of silver and bore a single tiny Honeystone set in a circle of pale blue Amelinas. It belonged to my mother and I shall be so terribly upset if I never see it again.' And she began to weep.

'Hush, my dear Mollinda,' said Captain Rufus kindly. 'I am sure that your ring cannot have been stolen, because no thief could possibly have gained entry to the castle. Maybe you accidentally dropped your ring on the floor. Come, let us all search your room carefully.'

And so they did. Crawling on all fours, Mollinda, Bellinda

and Captain Rufus swept their hands over every single inch of the floor. They lifted the rugs and looked underneath them. They peered under the bed and the dressing table. They even looked on top of the wardrobe. They searched and searched and searched – but of Mollinda's ring there was no trace.

'The door to my bedchamber was locked all night,' said Mollinda, 'and although I leave my window open just a little at night so that the sweet air, bearing the scent of the Sky-petal flowers, may enter, the gap was certainly not large enough to permit a thief to pass.'

Captain Rufus scratched his head. 'Well,' he said, 'I have to admit that the ring does not seem to be here. Perhaps it slipped off your finger and you did not notice. I shall go to ask everyone in the castle; someone may have found it.'

After he left Mollinda's bedchamber and was walking down the corridor, he met Old Joliphant the Butler.

'Ah, Captain Rufus,' said Old Joliphant, 'the very man I was looking for.'

'Good day, Master Joliphant,' said Captain Rufus, 'and how may I be of assistance to you?'

'Someone seems to have stolen one of my golden buttons,' said Old Joliphant. 'Each evening, when I supervise the King's dinner, I wear my best ceremonial tunic. This tunic bears twelve buttons of pure gold, given to me by King Ferdinand the Twelfth, the father of our dear King Ferdinand the Thirteenth. Each evening I carefully remove the buttons from my tunic so that I may polish them. Then, I place them in a small dish on the table that stands beside my bed. This morning there were only eleven buttons in the dish. One of them had gone.'

Captain Rufus went to Old Joliphant's room and, sure enough, only eleven buttons lay in the dish.

'I cannot understand it,' said Captain Rufus, frowning. ''Was your bedroom door locked?'

'Yes,' said Old Joliphant, 'I always lock my door at night.'

'And did you close your window?' asked Captain Rufus.

'It was not *quite* closed,' Old Joliphant replied. 'I like to keep it open just a little so that I may hear the evening song of the Moonbird and, in the morning, the call of the Dawnbird. But the gap was certainly not large enough to permit a thief to pass.'

'Well, this is all very strange,' said Captain Rufus. 'If it was indeed a thief who took your button, why did he only take *one* when he could have taken all twelve? Perhaps the button dropped off your tunic and you did not notice. I shall go and search for it throughout the castle.'

So saying, he left Old Joliphant's bedchamber. Presently, he met Alathéa, the Assistant Pastry Cook, a shy and pretty young maiden. Captain Rufus noticed that a small tear trickled slowly down her cheek.

'Good morrow, Mistress Alathéa,' said Captain Rufus, bowing courteously. 'Why – if I may be so bold as to enquire – do you weep?'

'Oh, Captain Rufus,' cried Alathéa, 'a thief entered the kitchen last night and stole the long pin, made of star-metal, that I use to prick the pastry before it is placed into the oven. I am so sad, because it was given to me by Wilhelmina the Cook.'

Captain Rufus went with Alathéa to the kitchen. Sure enough, the star-metal pin was nowhere to be found.

'I *know* that the kitchen door was locked,' said Alathéa, 'and though the window was left slightly ajar to allow the heat from the oven to escape into the night, the gap was not wide enough to permit a thief to pass.'

'Perhaps,' suggested Captain Rufus, 'the pin became caught in your apron and was carried to some other part of the castle. I shall go to look for it.'

And search he did, for hours and hours, all over the castle. Search as he might, however, Captain Rufus could not find Mollinda's silver ring, Old Joliphant's golden button, or Alathéa's star-metal pin, anywhere in the castle.

And not only *that*, but he learned that several other things had also been stolen during the night. From the room of Lady Cordelia, the Queen's chief Lady-in-Waiting, a tiny perfume bottle made of orange crystal had been taken; Roland the Servant reported that a jewelled buckle had gone from one of his shoes; and – worst of all – from Queen Berenice's favourite necklace, a magnificent Flame-diamond was missing.

Everyone said that the doors to their rooms had been locked all night. Though everyone had left their windows open just a little, no thief could possibly have entered that way, because the gaps were far too small.

When Captain Rufus told King Ferdinand about the thefts, the King stroked his chin and thought very hard.

'This is a most serious matter, Captain Rufus,' he said. 'I believe that there is only one person in the whole of Vàldovar who can help us to solve this great mystery. We must ride at once to consult the Wizard-who-lives-in-the-Wood.'

King Ferdinand and Captain Rufus commanded that their horses should be made ready. Within the hour, they were on their way. They rode for two days and two nights until they drew near to the great Wood of Wishing. There they found their way blocked. So many trees had grown during the spring, and so tight were the gaps between them, that there was no way into the wood. King Ferdinand did not hesitate. Riding forward, he raised his sword high and declared:

Wood of Wishing, tree and bush,
Bracken, fern, and reed and rush,
Ash and elm, and rowan tree,
Bow your heads, and welcome me.

He then spoke the magic word (quietly, so that Captain Rufus could not hear – for the magic word is secret, being known only to the Kings of Vàldovar and to very few others).

As soon as the trees heard the magic word, they moved slowly aside, leaving just enough room for King Ferdinand and Captain Rufus to ride between them.

They continued riding until they reached a clearing in the very heart of the wood, where stood the ancient oak tree. A huge carved door set into the trunk of the oak slowly opened, and out stepped the Wizard-who-lives-in-the-Wood. The blue moons on his tall, white, pointed hat glinted and glistened. On his blue cloak glittered silver stars.

'So, King Ferdinand the Thirteenth,' boomed the Wizard, 'you dare once more break the silence of the Wood of Wishing!'

Captain Rufus dismounted and strode forward. 'Sir Wizard,' he said, sternly, 'know that King Ferdinand is King of this Wood, just as he is King of all other secret places in Vàldovar. He *dares* go wherever it is his *desire* to go – and I, Rufus, Captain of the Guard, shall protect him.'

The Wizard smiled, and said: 'You speak well, Captain Rufus. Your valour is well-known to me.' Then, to King Ferdinand, he said: 'Tell me then, your Majesty, what brings you, yet again, to my wood?'

King Ferdinand explained that a thief must have entered

the royal castle, and had stolen a silver ring, a gold button, a star-metal pin, a crystal perfume bottle, a jewelled buckle, and – from the Queen's necklace – a precious Flame-diamond.'

'How could a thief have gained entry to the castle?' asked Captain Rufus. 'All the doors were locked, and, although windows were left slightly open, no thief could possibly have squeezed through such narrow gaps.'

The Wizard smiled. 'The solution to the mystery lies in the objects that were stolen,' he said. 'I know who is the thief.'

'Then tell me quickly,' said Captain Rufus, 'so that I may return and arrest the culprit.'

'The name of the thief,' replied the Wizard, 'is Gazzaladra. That was not difficult for me to work out. However,' he added, stroking his long, white beard thoughtfully, 'catching and arresting Gazzaladra will not be such a simple matter, for although I know his name, I do not know where he is hiding.'

'Then what are we to do?' cried King Ferdinand. 'We *must* find him and arrest him, or he will steal many more things from the royal castle.'

The Wizard thought for a few more moments and then he turned to Captain Rufus.

'Now listen carefully, Captain Rufus,' he said, 'and I shall tell you what must be done. You must enlist the aid of Mollinda the Chambermaid, for I have heard it said that she has a sweet and gentle voice. The day after you return to the royal castle, you and she must arise just as dawn is breaking, while the sky is still dark and the Morning Star may still be seen in the sky. Go both of you to the Whiteberry bush that grows outside the castle. There, spinning her daily web, you will find a little Morning Spider – her name is Aranéa. Hold out your hand, and let Aranéa drop gently upon it.

'Aranéa is shy and easily frightened, and so you must not speak to her in your deep, booming voice. Instead, ask Mollinda to sing softly to the little spider – and never fear, for she will know exactly what she must sing.'

'Then,' continued the Wizard, 'when Mollinda has sung her song, take Aranéa back to the royal castle and, that evening, place her carefully in a small box without a lid; then, beside her, lay *this*.'

From the folds of his robe, the Wizard drew a beautiful blue-green jewel that sparkled in the dappled sunlight. 'This,' said the Wizard, 'is an Aqualuna. Found only in the cold, dark, depths of faraway seas, where it alone shines, it is the rarest of all jewels, and more precious than diamonds.

'When you have done all these things, put the box containing Aranéa and the Aqualuna in an empty room. Lock the door of the room, but leave the window very slightly open (though not wide enough for anyone to enter by that way).'

Both Captain Rufus and King Ferdinand looked very puzzled. They could not see how singing to a spider, or locking a precious jewel in an empty room, could possibly help them catch a thief. Yet King Ferdinand knew that the Wizard was very clever and that his suggestions usually gave the right result in the end, so he said to Captain Rufus: 'Come, my friend, let us go and do as the great Wizard bids,' and, after thanking the Wizard-who-lives-in-the-Wood, they rode back to the royal castle.

On the morning after his return, Captain Rufus arose, as usual, just before dawn. He dressed quickly, then hurried to the castle gate, where (as she had been instructed) Mollinda was already waiting for him. Together, they went out of the castle to find the Whiteberry bush. The first red rays of the rising sun were beginning to appear, but overhead the sky remained dark. Low down in the sky, the Morning Star still twinkled.

Captain Rufus and Mollinda saw that a beautiful, delicate web had been spun on the Whiteberry bush, and that, dangling from the web, on a fine thread of gossamer, was a tiny Morning Spider. The spider was grey-green in colour, with delicate white markings on its back. Captain Rufus knew (because the Wizard had told him) that the spider's name was Aranéa. Captain Rufus held out his hand and, loosening her grip on the gossamer thread, Aranéa dropped gently into his palm.

'Sing now to Aranéa,' Captain Rufus said to Mollinda.

'Sing the words that come into your heart.' Putting her face close to the little spider, Mollinda sang softly (though whence the words of her song came, she could not – then or afterwards – say):

I greet thee, Aranéa,
In the cold of early morn,
Where, on diamond dew around us,
Strike the rosy threads of dawn.

Under sky that holds its darkness,
'Neath the star that lingers yet,
The finger of the breeze bestirs
Thy new-built spid'ry net.

With gossamer and starlight,
Thou thy lacy home hast spun,
Through the dark of night-time toiling,
'Til the rising of the sun.

Now hear me, Aranéa,
For I speak of my belief
That thy skills that caught the starlight
May be used to catch a thief.

So I call upon the magic
Of the morning – for I'm told
That a spell that's cast in dawnlight
Has the pow'r to summon gold.

Gold to clothe thee, Aranéa,
And to gild thy silken bed,
Gold to glisten when the starlight
Falls upon thy golden thread.

As soon as Mollinda's song had ended, a very strange thing happened. The spider changed colour from grey-green to a wonderful, shining gold!

Captain Rufus and Mollinda returned quickly to the castle, the Captain carrying Aranéa carefully back to his room where he kept her until evening. Then, as night was falling, he took her to an empty bedroom and put her gently into a small box with no lid. Into the box he placed also the Aqualuna that the Wizard had given to him.

Finally, he put the box onto a small table near to the door, opened a window *very* slightly (not wide enough for anyone to climb through) and, after leaving the room, locked the door behind him with a big iron key.

Later, in the middle of the night, when everyone else in the castle was sound asleep, Captain Rufus crept back to the empty bedroom where he had left Aranéa and the Aqualuna. Carefully, he unlocked the door with the big iron key, and looked inside the room.

The first thing he saw was that the little box that he had left on the table just inside the room was empty. Aranéa had gone, and *so had the precious Aqualuna*! The thief had somehow managed to get into the room and steal it.

With a gasp, Captain Rufus threw open the door and ran into the room. Then he stopped. Arising out of the box where the Aqualuna had been, there was a fine, golden thread which shone and sparkled.

Captain Rufus realized immediately what had happened. During the night, Aranéa had started to spin her web. When the thief had taken the Aqualuna, Aranéa must have clung to it whilst continuing to produce her gossamer thread which – like Aranéa herself – was made of gold so pure that it could be seen at night in the light of the stars and moon.

The gossamer thread led from the box, up into the air, across the room and …. Captain Rufus could hardly believe his eyes! The thread passed through the narrow gap in the open window and out into the night.

Quickly, Captain Rufus ran down the stairs and out of the castle. Looking up, he could see, gleaming and glinting clearly, the golden thread. It came out of the bedroom window, passed high across the castle moat, and then disappeared into the dense branches of a large birch tree.

Captain Rufus did not hesitate. He ran to the tree and started to climb. He could see, far above him, the golden gossamer thread glinting amongst the leaves. Finally he reached it. Following it with his eyes, he saw that it led into a bird's nest, and, standing on the branch at the side of the nest, was a large, black and white *magpie*!

Captain Rufus looked at the magpie, and the magpie looked at Captain Rufus.

'Who are you,' asked the magpie, 'and what do you want? This is *my* tree and I prefer not to be disturbed.'

'Oh,' said Captain Rufus, very surprised to find a magpie who could talk. 'Well, I'm Captain Rufus, and I'm Captain of the Guard. And who, might I ask, are you?'

'My name is Gazzaladra,' replied the magpie, and Captain Rufus recalled that the Wizard-who-lives-in-the-Wood had said that this was the name of the thief. Then, he saw that woven into the very fabric of Gazzaladra's nest were a silver ring, a gold button, a star-metal pin, a jewelled buckle, a crystal perfume bottle, a twinkling Flame-diamond, *and* a beautiful blue-green Aqualuna – everything, in fact, that had been stolen from the castle.

Of course! Only a thief as small as a bird could have squeezed through the narrow gaps that had been left in the open windows.

Captain Rufus suddenly remembered – magpies are *well-known* thieves! The gentleman magpie will steal anything that is bright and shiny, so that he can put it in the nest that he has made. Then, when a lady magpie sees that his nest has been so very beautifully decorated, she will think to herself: 'What a fine magpie this must be to have such a grand nest!' And if the lady magpie is *very* impressed she may even decide to marry the gentleman magpie. For such is the way of the world.

Captain Rufus reached out his hand towards Gazzaladra's nest and from it picked out all the stolen objects.

At first, Gazzaladra was extremely upset about this, and he squeaked and squawked and flapped his wings. But then he saw that Aranéa had continued to spin her web on his nest. The golden gossamer thread, and the wonderfully intricate web, made Gazzaladra's nest sparkle and shine in the moonlight. It was *beautiful*!

From high above, came the voice of a lady magpie who had spotted the twinkling nest.

I think it's best
If a magpie's nest
With gossamer can shine.
The one I see,
(It seems to me)
Is perfect to be mine.

So down I'll fly,
And offer my
Affections to the one
Whose nest of gold
Will surely hold
A life second to none.

He must be fine
If his nest can shine
So twinklingly at night.
Yes, he will be,
For a bird like me,
A husband who's just right!

So the lady magpie flew down to the nest. Gazzaladra was so delighted when he saw how pretty she was that he quite forgot about the stolen jewels and other shiny things that he had used to decorate his nest.

Captain Rufus took all the stolen objects back to the castle and, next morning, handed them to their rightful owners. Everyone, of course, was delighted, and they all thought that Captain Rufus was not only *very* clever, but that he was the best Captain of the Guard there had ever been.

Back in the Wood of Wishing, a beautiful black-and-white magpie flew down into the clearing where stood the Wizard-who-lives-in-the-Wood. It was Gazzaladra!

Gazzaladra marched up and down on the grass (as magpies do) in front of the Wizard and told him of all that had happened.

Mollinda had put her ring back on her finger and vowed never to take it off again. Old Joliphant had put back the gold button with the eleven others and always kept them in a locked box when they were not safely on his tunic. Alathéa kept her star-metal pin in the waist-band of her apron, so that she always knew where to find it. Cordelia locked her perfume bottle in a drawer of her dressing table. Roland made sure that his buckles were always well sewn on to his shoes. And Dornadel, the Royal Jeweller, fixed the Flame-diamond securely back into Queen Berenice's necklace.

In his beak, Gazzaladra carried the blue-green Aqualuna, which he placed carefully on the ground at the Wizard's feet.

'King Ferdinand bade me return this to you, Lord Wizard,' said Gazzaladra, 'and to thank you for your help.'

The Wizard looked sternly at Gazzaladra. 'I trust, my dear fellow, that you will never again steal *anything* from the royal castle,' he said.

'It shall be as you command, my Lord,' replied Gazzaladra. 'This will not be a problem, for my friend Aranéa has decided to make her home on my nest, and her golden web that she must spin anew each day makes it more splendid than any jewel could achieve. And, in any case, I now have a beautiful wife called Pica-Pica who, because of my fine golden nest, loves me very much indeed.'

'Hmm,' said the Wizard thoughtfully, 'I think that you should make sure that Aranéa *remains* your friend.'

Gazzaladra bowed and then, with a flap of his wings, flew away, out of the Wood of Wishing and back to his nest in the birch tree, where Pica-Pica sat on three speckled eggs.

'Ah!' sighed the Wizard, 'strange are the ways of magpies and men.'

Then, stroking his long, white beard, smiling a little smile, and shaking his head, the Wizard-who-lives-in-the-Wood went back into his home in the ancient oak. Behind him, the great carved door swung shut.

The Cook

O ne fine summer's day, long ago, King Ferdinand the Thirteenth, King of Vàldovar, and his wife, the beautiful Queen Berenice, were walking together in the garden of their castle, admiring the flowers and listening to the songs of the birds, when one of the servants approached them.

'I beg to inform your Majesties,' said the servant, 'that a Messenger has just arrived and would speak with you.'

King Ferdinand and Queen Berenice returned to the castle, and took their places on the golden thrones in the great hall. The Messenger stood before the King.

'Your Majesty,' he said, bowing low, 'her Highness the Duchess of Gath wishes to inform you that, in five days' time, she will arrive to pay you a visit, and that she, her husband and their son, will stay with you for a week.'

'Return to the Duchess,' replied the King, 'and tell her that we shall, as always, be delighted and honoured to receive her and her family as our guests.'

'As you command, Sire,' said the Messenger and, after

again bowing to King Ferdinand and Queen Berenice, he left the throne room.

As soon as the Messenger had gone, King Ferdinand buried his head in his hands and groaned.

'Oh no!' he moaned. 'I really don't think I can stand it.'

Now let me explain why poor King Ferdinand was so appalled by the thought that the Duchess of Gath was coming to stay for a whole week.

The Duchess was also King Ferdinand's Aunt Clarissa, and so she naturally assumed that she could come to stay with her nephew whenever she wished. She was a very large lady who never spoke quietly. The boom of her voice, echoing round the castle, always gave King Ferdinand the most terrible headache. Not only that, but whenever she visited the castle she complained about simply *everything*. She complained that the rooms were too cold (or too hot), that the beds were too hard (or too soft), that the weather was too wet (or too dry), and that the food had too much salt (or too little).

Everyone always tried very hard to please her, but no-one ever succeeded. If King Ferdinand and his Aunt were walking in the garden, and King Ferdinand happened to say, 'See what a beautiful day it is, Aunt Clarissa,' she would peer sternly at him through her lorgnette and declare: 'Well *you* might think that this is fine weather, but *I* find it unbearably windy, and I am sure that I just felt spots of rain.'

To make matters even worse, the Duchess was always accompanied by her small, timid husband, Otho, and their whining son, Waldo. Whenever she complained about anything, Otho would say to her: 'You are quite right, my dear.' And Waldo would say in his squeaky voice: 'Yes, mother, I agree with you, too. *Everything* in this castle is absolutely *awful*.'

And so you can understand why King Ferdinand was not looking forward to having the Duchess and her family in the castle for a whole week.

'Is there nothing we can do,' he asked Queen Berenice, 'to persuade them not to come?'

'No, my dear,' Queen Berenice replied. 'We must always be hospitable. The Duchess, your Aunt, has announced her intention to pay us a visit, and that is that. We shall just have to make the best of it.'

'Yes, I suppose you are right,' said King Ferdinand. 'Well, we have only five days in which to prepare, so we had better start straight away.'

Queen Berenice agreed. 'I shall go to tell Wilhelmina the Cook to prepare her most special dishes,' she said, 'so that the Duchess and her family will find it very difficult to complain about the meals.'

When Queen Berenice went to the castle kitchen, however, Wilhelmina the Cook was nowhere to be found.

'Oh, your Majesty,' said Hilda the Kitchen Maid,

'Wilhelmina is now so elderly, and her eyesight is so poor, that she is no longer able to cook. She has returned to the village where she was born, there to live quietly with her sister. This lies five days' journey to the north, in the green hills of Ethren.'

'Oh dear,' said Queen Berenice, 'I had quite forgotten. What *are* we to do? The Duchess of Gath and her family will arrive in five days' time and there is no-one else in the castle who can prepare such wonderful dishes as those cooked by Wilhelmina.'

Just as the Queen was saying this, the kitchen door opened, and a young man entered. It was Archibald the Stableboy, who looked after the King's horses. Now, Archibald was the son of Wilhelmina the Cook.

'Excuse me, your Majesty,' Archibald said. 'I overheard what you said, and I think that I could be of service to you and his Majesty, King Ferdinand.'

'In what way?' asked the Queen in surprise.

'Well,' replied Archibald, 'I often watched my mother, Wilhelmina the Cook, when she was cooking, and can remember perfectly what she did. I am sure that I could take her place.'

'Oh,' said Queen Berenice, 'that would be wonderful! I shall let the King know of your kindness.'

When King Ferdinand learned of Archibald's offer to do the cooking, he was very pleased. 'You see, my dear,' he said to Queen Berenice, 'how the good people of Vàldovar are ever ready and willing to help others. We are truly fortunate to be King and Queen of such a land.'

Down in the kitchen, meanwhile, Archibald immediately set to work to prepare the dishes for that evening's dinner. He called together all the Assistant Cooks (there were twelve of them) and told them what he needed.

'I shall require lots of flour,' said Archibald, 'and at least a jugful of vinegar. Then I need a dozen apples, some eggs, and a large bunch of watercress.'

As he continued listing the ingredients of the dishes he would prepare, the Assistant Cooks scratched their heads.

'I cannot see what kind of meal you could possibly make with these things,' one of them said, and the others agreed.

Archibald, however, merely laughed. 'I know exactly what I'm doing,' he said. 'I can recall perfectly how my mother, Wilhelmina, used to cook.' Then he frowned. 'Or at least I *think* I can.'

Although the Assistant Cooks were not at all sure that Archibald knew the first thing about cooking, they did as he said and brought him the ingredients for which he had asked. Archibald worked all afternoon, frying and baking, boiling and stewing, and by evening everything was ready.

In the great dining hall, King Ferdinand and Queen Berenice sat with their daughter, Princess Ianthe, their son, Prince Almeric, and Almeric's wife, the Princess Britta.

Around the table the courtiers and palace officials, and others who worked in the castle, took their places.

'Tonight,' King Ferdinand announced, 'is a special occasion. It is the first dinner prepared by Archibald, son of Wilhelmina. I now name him Archibald the Cook. His mother was known throughout Vàldovar for the excellence of her cooking, and I am told that Archibald remembers well her famous recipes. I am sure that we are all to be treated to one of the most remarkable meals ever served in Vàldovar.'

It turned out that King Ferdinand was absolutely correct – but not quite in the way that he had expected.

The Royal Bugler sounded a fanfare, the doors of the great dining hall opened, and in marched the Assistant Cooks, each carrying a large pot from which steam arose. With long ladles, the Assistant Cooks put food out of the pots onto the plates, and the diners looked at it.

'What *is* it?' whispered the Lady Cordelia, the Queen's chief Lady-in-Waiting.

Humbert, the King's Secretary, peered at the food on his plate. 'I've no idea,' he said. 'I don't think I've ever seen anything quite like it. It smells a bit like some kind of meat, but it can't be because it's black. And I can't think what these round green things are. They look rather like peas, but they are much too hard.'

All round the table, people were poking at the food with

their knives and forks.

'Come, my friends,' King Ferdinand said. 'We may not recognize what is in this dish, but that does not mean that it is not delicious.' So saying, he took up his knife and fork and placed some of the food into his mouth.

Everyone watched. A very strange look came over the King's face. First his eyes grew wide, and then he shut them tightly. Next, his cheeks bulged, and his face became bright red. Finally, with a great gulp he swallowed, seized a glass of water, drank the whole lot, and then lay back in his chair, gasping.

'Well!' said the Lady Cordelia. 'This must be really delicious food for it to have such a wonderful effect upon King Ferdinand.' And so everyone started eagerly to eat.

Soon, they were all gasping and spluttering. Princess Britta ran from the room, her hand over her mouth. Prince Almeric lay on his back on the floor, holding up a water jug and pouring the water into his open mouth. Queen Berenice was trying to speak, but seemed unable to produce any sound. All around the room, people sat with their heads on the table, or rolled about on the floor holding their stomachs.

Gradually, the effect of the food wore off, and all the diners sat in silence, leaving the rest of the meal untouched. Then Roland the Servant started to sing a little song, and soon everyone joined in. This is what they sang:

When the one who does the stewing
Doesn't know what he is doing,
And the meat is all burnt and black;
When the food that's on the table
Can't be eaten (we're not able!),
Then the cook must be given the sack.
Let us sack him,
Oh yes, sack him,
And we'll send all this dreadful food back
To the cook who tried to bake it
And we'll tell him he should take it
To the piglets – then we'll give him the sack.
Yes, we'll sack him,
Oh, we'll sack him.
We'll make sure that he's given the sack!

King Ferdinand called for silence.

'My friends,' he said, 'I agree with you all that this is easily the worst meal that any of us has ever eaten, and quite possibly it is the worst meal that has ever been prepared in the history of the world. However, we must remember that in Vàldovar we should always be kind, and never, *ever*, say or do anything to hurt another person's feelings. Archibald offered to become the Cook simply because he wanted to help your King Ferdinand and your Queen Berenice. He was very kind to us, and we must be kind to him. We *cannot* say to him that his cooking is dreadful. We must tell him that it is excellent.'

The others groaned, but they knew that King Ferdinand was right. They could not be unkind to Archibald, who had, after all, only been trying to be helpful.

'But,' someone called out, 'does that mean that we actually have to *eat* it?'

'Well, yes, I rather fear it does,' said King Ferdinand, and so, pulling the most awful faces, that is what everyone did. They closed their eyes and held their noses, and then, slowly and painfully, munched, chewed and gulped their way through the rest of the meal.

When, later that evening, Archibald the Cook asked King Ferdinand what everyone had thought of the dinner, King Ferdinand replied: 'No-one had ever tasted anything like it. It was very … er … *unusual*.'

Archibald smiled happily. 'I am so pleased that you liked it,' he said. 'I have some even better recipes planned for tomorrow.'

'Oh, my goodness,' said King Ferdinand (quietly – so as not to upset Archibald), 'I was afraid of that.'

The next day, as Archibald once more prepared the royal food, he hummed the recipes to himself. Just to show you what Archibald's cooking was really like, here is one of his recipes.

Take a pinch (just a pinch) of powdery pepper
And sprinkle it, sparingly, into a pan.
Crack an egg (a brown egg) and whisk it up quickly,
Then make it with sugar as sweet as you can.

Choose a pear (a ripe pear) and slice it up thinly,
And carefully add to the goo that you've got.
Put the pan (the bright pan) onto the fire;
Keep stirring the mixture until it is hot.

When the smoke (the black smoke) is starting to billow,
Remove from the fire before it's too late!
With a knife (a sharp knife) cut it up into slices,
Then tip it out onto a white china plate.

Add some milk (creamy milk) and juice from a lemon,
Some peas and some carrots, and bits of cold meat.
In a pot (iron pot) you should thoroughly boil it,
Then stir in some jam – and it's ready to eat!

Take it and
Taste it and
Munch it and
Crunch it and
Suck it and
Chew it and
Then, if you would,

Nip it and
Bite it and
Gnaw it and
Grind it and
Lick it and
Lap it and
Tell me it's good!

Upstairs, in the throne room, King Ferdinand and Queen Berenice sat miserably on their golden thrones.

The King rested his chin in his hands, and looked at the Queen. 'Do you realize,' he said glumly, 'that the Duchess of Gath (my Aunt Clarissa) will be here in only four days' time? And I shudder – I absolutely *shudder* – to think what she and her ghastly husband and even ghastlier son will have to say about the meals. She will make my life even more miserable than it already is. What can we possibly do?'

Queen Berenice thought carefully, and then she brightened up. '*I* know!' she cried. 'We shall go at once to speak to the Wizard-who-lives-in-the-Wood. He is the only one who can help us.'

King Ferdinand agreed, and so, without more ado, horses were made ready and the King and Queen set out. They rode for two days and two nights until eventually they reached the Wood of Wishing.

There they found that it was impossible to enter the wood, because tall spikes of Swordgrass and dense tangles of Spikybriar barred the way. King Ferdinand, however, rode forward and said:

Wood of Wishing, hear my call;
Lower now thy leafy wall.
With the Wizard I would talk,
And down thy sylvan paths must walk.

He then spoke the magic word that is known only to the Kings of Vàldovar and to few others (Queen Berenice was one of those who knew what it was). Slowly, the Swordgrass became limp and lay flat upon the ground. The Spikybriar became untangled, and drew to one side. The way into the Wood of Wishing was now clear, and a leafy path, leading to the very centre of the wood, lay ahead.

The King and Queen rode into the wood until they reached a clearing where there grew a mighty oak tree, larger than any other in the whole world. A huge door in the oak tree opened, and out stepped the Wizard-who-lives-in-the-Wood, his long blue cloak, and his tall, pointed white hat, glimmering with silver stars and blue moons.

'I am honoured that both King Ferdinand and the fair Queen Berenice come to visit my ancient wood,' said the Wizard, 'even though my trees do not like being woken from their deep sleep by the magic word.'

King Ferdinand then told the Wizard about Archibald the Cook and about the terrible meals that he prepared. He also explained that he did not wish to upset Archibald by telling him just how bad his cooking really was.

'And,' added the King, 'the Duchess of Gath is arriving with Otho, her husband, and Waldo, their son, in only two days' time, and we cannot *possibly* give them the kind of meals that Archibald cooks.'

The Wizard stroked his long, white beard and thought very, very carefully. Then he smiled.

'Yes,' he said at last, 'I think I know what can be done. Tell me, Queen Berenice, do you know whether any of the Assistant Cooks has a special love of flowers?'

'Well, yes,' replied the Queen. 'Alathéa, a shy young maid who works in the kitchen as Assistant Pastry Cook, is often to be seen gathering flowers in the woods. She knows them all by their Valdovarian names.'

'Then,' said the Wizard, 'this is what you must do.'

From within the folds of his blue cloak he withdrew a small, round mirror, the rim of which was fashioned in pure gold.

'Take this mirror and give it to Alathéa. Tell her that she should go quickly to the fields and woodlands and there gather only those flowers that seem to glow with a golden light when reflected in this mirror. Flowers that do not glow when viewed in the mirror she is to leave.'

King Ferdinand and Queen Berenice were surprised.

'And what is Alathéa to do with the flowers that she collects?' asked the King.

'Ah,' replied the Wizard, 'you may safely leave that to Alathéa. She will know *exactly* what needs to be done.'

Still puzzled, and wondering how the Wizard's advice could possibly help, King Ferdinand and Queen Berenice rode for two days and two nights, returning to their castle on the same day that the Duchess and her family were to arrive.

They found that everyone looked thoroughly miserable, because for the past four days they had all been eating Archibald's meals, and these had become worse and worse as each day passed.

The King and Queen gave the Wizard's mirror to Alathéa, and bade her do quickly as the Wizard had said.

Alathéa curtsied. 'I shall do as you command, your Majesties,' she said, and, taking the mirror, she hurried out forthwith into the fields and woodlands around the castle.

Each time that she came upon a flower, she looked at it through the mirror, and was astonished to find that some flowers shimmered and glowed with a strange golden light when reflected in the glass, whilst others did not. Remembering what the King and Queen had said, she gathered only those that glowed in the mirror.

As she put the flowers into the basket that she carried, she began to realize that, in addition to the natural perfume of each flower, there were also new scents that she had never noticed before. The pink Maidenblush smelt faintly of roast potatoes; the yellow Sunblossom had about it the smell of bacon sizzling in the pan; from the orange Dawnrose came the odour of hot apple pie and custard; and there arose from the purple flower of the Emperor's Robe a delicious aroma of freshly-baked bread. An idea gradually formed in Alathéa's mind.

As soon as she had filled her basket with flowers she hurried back to the kitchen where Archibald the Cook was busy stirring a bowl full of something thick and green that smelt really *horrible*. Bubbling away in a large pot on the fire was a bright red liquid – and *that* smelt even worse. From a large joint of meat which lay on a platter, blue smoke curled up to the kitchen ceiling. A bowl contained a pile of vegetables that had been boiled for so long that they had gone all soggy.

'This,' said Archibald to all the Assistant Cooks who were looking with horror at the ruined food, 'will be one of the finest meals that anyone has ever tasted. Our honoured guests, the Duchess of Gath, her husband, the Lord Otho, and Waldo, their son, will, I am sure, be delighted.'

Everyone really wanted to tell Archibald that his food was so awful that it could not possibly be served up for dinner – and certainly not to King Ferdinand's Aunt and her family –

but they remembered that King Ferdinand had forbidden them to say anything that would hurt the Cook's feelings, and so they remained dutifully silent.

After a while, Archibald and the Assistant Cooks went to prepare the dining table – except for Alathéa, who was left alone in the kitchen. Quickly, she went to the dreadful dishes that Archibald the Cook had prepared, and onto each she scattered a few petals from the flowers in her basket.

To the thick, green soup she added a few red Fire Daisy petals; onto the red, bubbling sauce in the pot she sprinkled the tiny pink petals of the Sunrise Lily; and onto the burnt and blackened meat a handful of white Snowflower petals. Petals from other flowers were added to the soggy vegetables, to the hard and unchewable bread, to pies whose dark and singed crusts covered goodness-knows-what, and to any other food that had been prepared for dinner.

Later that evening, King Ferdinand and Queen Berenice took their places at table. Beside the King sat the Duchess of Gath, while her husband, Otho, and her son, Waldo, sat next to Queen Berenice.

'I expect,' said the Duchess, 'that this will be a very poor dinner – as usual.'

'I am sure you are right, my dear,' said her husband Otho.

'Yes, mother,' squeaked her son Waldo, 'you are *always* right. The food here is never as good as it is in our own castle.'

'I am afraid,' King Ferdinand whispered to Queen Berenice, 'that for once the Duchess will, indeed, be proved right. I dread to think what she will say when she is faced with Archibald's cooking.'

At that moment, the Royal Bugler sounded the fanfare and the first course was served.

The Duchess stared at the thick green liquid in the bowl that had been placed in front of her.

'And what, pray, is this?' she demanded.

'I'm not sure,' replied King Ferdinand, 'but I think it is some kind of soup.'

'Well, whatever it is, it looks quite revolting,' said the Duchess. Then she took a spoon, scooped up a small amount of the green liquid, and popped it into her mouth.

Everyone in the room went completely silent. No-one dared to speak. They all simply watched and waited. Whatever would the Duchess say? Whatever would she do? Would she scream, clutch her stomach and run from the room? Would she pick up the bowl of green goo and tip it over King Ferdinand's head? A few people covered their eyes with their hands because they could not bear to see what dreadful thing was going to happen next.

Then, everyone gasped in amazement. The Duchess started to smile. Yes – she *actually smiled*!

Turning to King Ferdinand, she announced: 'Well, my

dear King Ferdinand, I must say that this is the most wonderful soup that I have ever tasted in my whole life. It is so delicate of flavour! So perfect of texture! You surely have the best Cook in the whole of Vàldovar.'

'Er … well I … well, yes, I do believe that Archibald the Cook is very … umm … *inventive*,' King Ferdinand stammered, utterly astonished.

Everyone round the table then carefully tasted a little of the soup and, to their complete surprise, found that what the Duchess had said was perfectly true. The soup was delicious!

When the empty dishes had been cleared away, the Royal Bugler again sounded a fanfare. In came the Assistant Cooks bearing platters of smoking, burnt meat, soggy vegetables, and an evil-smelling red sauce.

'Oh, my goodness,' groaned King Ferdinand, burying his head in his hands. 'This looks quite disgusting.'

The Duchess, however, tucked into the food as though she had not had a decent meal for weeks, and so too did Otho and Waldo. They hacked eagerly at the meat, and crammed great chunks of it into their mouths. They chomped and chewed and swallowed. Then they spooned up the soggy vegetables and ate them with every sign of enjoyment.

When King Ferdinand and Queen Berenice tried the meat, they had to agree that it really was excellent. Although it looked as though it would be as tough as a leather saddle, it was tender, juicy, and cooked to perfection. The vegetables, too, were firm and flavoursome, despite their soggy, overboiled appearance.

'Excellent!' announced the Duchess, as she finished off the last of the vegetables, and used a chunk of what looked like rock-hard bread to soak up the last of the red sauce. 'Perfect!'

And so it continued. As course after course was served, each looking dreadful but tasting delicious, the Duchess smiled more and more, and even her husband, Otho, and their appalling son, Waldo, complimented King Ferdinand on the excellence of the cooking.

For the next seven days, the food continued to be wonderful, and when the time came for the Duchess, her husband, Otho, and their son, Waldo, to return to their own home, they were full of smiles, and they thanked King Ferdinand and Queen Berenice for the wonderful meals that had been served.

'I wonder, King Ferdinand,' said the Duchess, 'whether you would be kind enough to allow your Cook to come back to our castle with us for a few days. Upon our return we wish to have a great feast for our friends and relatives, to show them all what food should *really* taste like.'

'Certainly,' replied the King. 'I shall command Archibald the Cook to accompany you.'

The following day, after the Duchess and her family had

departed, taking Archibald the Cook with them, Alathéa, the Assistant Cook, came to the throne room where King Ferdinand and Queen Berenice sat. She confessed to them how she had sprinkled the flower petals onto Archibald's dishes.

'I just knew,' she said, 'that flowers with such wonderful perfumes would make even the worst and most badly-prepared food taste delicious.'

Queen Berenice stared in horror at King Ferdinand. 'But,' she said, 'when Archibald prepares the food for the feast that the Duchess is arranging for her friends and relatives, Alathéa will not be there to sprinkle her flower petals upon it and …'

'And,' said King Ferdinand, 'it will taste absolutely awful!'

'*And*,' added Queen Berenice, 'it also means that the Duchess will never again be able to say that everything in her castle is better than it is in ours.'

King Ferdinand and Queen Berenice began to smile. Their smiles grew broader and broader and then they started to laugh and laugh. They laughed so much that tears streamed down their faces, and they almost fell off their thrones.

And, of course, the food that Archibald cooked for the Duchess's feast was indeed so dreadful that all the Duchess's friends and relatives ran out of the dining room, coughing and spluttering.

Archibald was immediately sent back to King Ferdinand,

where he announced that he seemed to have lost his interest in cooking, and that he now thought he would rather not be the Royal Cook. He asked whether he might be allowed to return to being the Stableboy once more. King Ferdinand and Queen Berenice were only too happy to agree to this.

Alathéa was appointed Royal Cook. Every day, she would go out into the fields and woods and there collect only those flowers that glowed when reflected in the Wizard's magic mirror. (She knew that any flower that did not glow in the mirror might be bitter and taste horrid – no matter how pretty it looked – and, if added to food, could make you very poorly.)

Thus, with the mirror's help, Alathéa produced the most wonderful dishes, and became known as the best Cook in the whole of Vàldovar.

Back in the Wood of Wishing, a tiny wren flew down into the clearing where stood the Wizard-who-lives-in-the-Wood. Perching on the Wizard's shoulder, the wren twittered and chirped into his ear.

She told him how Alathéa had gathered flowers that were reflected in the magic mirror, and had then sprinkled their petals onto the food that Archibald had prepared, and how this had transformed the food, making it delicious.

She told him, too, that Archibald had produced really dreadful food for the feast to which the Duchess had invited all her very important friends. Indeed, it had been so awful, that the Duchess no longer complained about *anything* that other people did.

Finally, the little wren explained how Archibald had returned to the work he really enjoyed in the Royal stables, and how Alathéa had been appointed Royal Cook.

Like King Ferdinand and Queen Berenice, the Wizard, too, began to smile and smile, and then to laugh and laugh. He laughed so hard that he almost fell over and had to use his wooden staff to stay on his feet.

Then, from far away, came faintly the sound of singing. The Wizard put a hand to his ear and listened carefully. Floating across the meadows, over the gentle hills and through the sun-dappled valleys, came the sweet voice of Alathéa. And this is the song that she sang:

> *The flowers of the woodland,*
> *And the flowers in the grass,*
> *The flowers on the hillside,*
> *Mirrored in the magic glass,*
> *Hold within their pretty petals*
> *A transforming floral spell*
> *That by others is forgotten,*
> *Though a Wizard knows it well.*

This magic is not talked of,
And is written in no book,
But, reflected in a mirror,
Is detected by a Cook.
If the petals from the flowers
Are just sprinkled on a dish,
Then the cooking will taste better
Than the best of Cooks could wish.

So remember when you see them,
Where in woods and fields they grow,
That the sweetly scented flowers
May a tasteful magic know.
If their brightly glowing petals
In the magic glass are seen,
They will surely grace the cooking
For a Royal King and Queen.

The song faded away, and the little wren flew from the Wizard's shoulder, up into the trees, and away.

Still laughing, and humming the tune to Alathéa's song, the Wizard-who-lives-in-the-Wood turned and walked back into his home in the ancient oak. Behind him, the great carved door swung shut.

The Conjuror

s you know, very few people from other lands ever visit Vàldovar. This is not only because it cannot be found on any map, but also because the country is bounded by high, snow-covered mountains, deep, deep forests, and the stormy sea.

Once, however, many, many years ago, in the reign of King Ferdinand the Thirteenth, a stranger *did* come to Vàldovar, and this is the story of how he came and what he did – and why, even today, the people of Vàldovar still speak of him.

It happened like this.

One bright, clear morning, Aethrid the Watchman was in his watchtower on one of the high cliffs of Vàldovar, looking out over the sea. It was his task to keep a lookout for storm clouds and to warn the people of approaching bad weather.

In fact, Aethrid had very little to do, because the weather was never bad in Vàldovar. Rain, when it came, was always gentle and never lasted very long – just long enough to water the flowers and keep the streams and lakes filled.

In the short winter, of course, the snow fell, and this was

a time that the children loved. But no-one could ever remember a foggy day, or a day when the sky was grey or the wind cold.

Aethrid actually spent most of his time watching the gulls wheeling and calling in the clear sky, and the porposies leaping in the sea far below the cliff where the watchtower stood.

On this particular day, Aethrid was enjoying the spectacle of a shoal of hundreds of Winged Fish that skimmed just above the waves before plunging once more into the depths of the sea. Suddenly, he spotted something, far, far away – something that seemed to be floating in the air.

At first it was just a small dot in the sky, but gradually the dot became bigger and bigger as the object drew closer and closer to land.

When, at last, Aethrid could make out what it was, he could hardly believe his eyes.

A huge balloon was floating, high in the sky, and was coming towards him. The balloon was yellow, with wonderful patterns of orange and red around it. Hanging beneath the balloon was a round basket, and inside the basket stood a man.

But what a strange man he was! His skin was dark, his eyes deep brown, and his jet-black hair hung in a long plait. He had a short, pointed beard that turned up at the tip.

He wore a fine scarlet robe, and on his head was something that had never before been seen in Vàldovar, and so the Valdovarians had no word for it. We would call it a *turban*: it was a long band of red silk that wound round and round and over and over the stranger's head so many times that it bulged out at the sides and on top. Across the turban, and down the front of the splendid scarlet robe, were bands of paler silk on which were sewn wonderful jewels which sparkled and flashed in the clear morning sunlight.

The balloon, and the basket with the stranger in it, passed right over Aethrid's watchtower. Aethrid scrambled down the twisting stairs and out of his tower.

He ran after the balloon, shouting: 'Stop, stop, stop!' (But *how*, I wonder, did he expect the stranger to stop? Balloons don't have any brakes – at least, not the kind of balloons that *I've* ever seen.)

Anyway, whether his balloon had any brakes or not, the stranger did not stop, but simply smiled and waved down to Aethrid.

Aethrid followed the balloon, until at last they came to a village. As soon the villagers caught sight of the wonderful balloon and the oddly-dressed stranger in the basket that hung from it, they rushed out from their houses and shouted and waved.

Then, very slowly, the balloon began to descend. As it drew closer to them, the villagers could hear the stranger singing. This is what he sang.

Oh, my name is Sharla-Tana;
I have flown across the sea,
Bringing magic spells and potions
From the land of Araby.

From my hat I can pull rabbits,
From my sleeve a speckled hen;
I can tell a lady's fortune,
And the destiny of men.

I have books with moving pictures,
I have necklaces that glow
In the glooming of the evening.
And your secret thoughts I know.

I can take away your worries,
I can soothe your deepest fear,
And if you should have a problem
I can make it disappear.

So come all you kindly people,
Gather round and you will see
All the wonders of the magic
That I bring from Araby.

At last, the basket came to rest on the grass and the stranger stepped out.

He was very tall – far taller, in fact, than anyone the villagers had ever seen. The villagers stood with their mouths open, gazing in wonder at Sharla-Tana's large turban which sported a fine plume, and at his silken clothes – and particularly at his red pointed shoes with their curly, turned-up tips.

No-one spoke a word. Then Sharla-Tana bowed low, straightened up again, and said, in a loud, deep voice: 'Behold!'

He put his hand behind his back and, when he withdrew it, he was holding an enormous bunch of big, bright-pink flowers.

The villagers gasped in astonishment. 'Ooooh!' they said, and 'Aaaah!'

'Where did *they* come from?' exclaimed Loxley the Archer.

Then Sharla-Tana tossed the flowers high into the air. Up and up they went, turning over and over, until suddenly, with a loud *pop*! they completely disappeared in a small puff of white smoke.

There were no more 'Ooohs' and 'Aaahs' from the crowd. Producing a bunch of flowers from behind your back is *surprising*, certainly, but making them disappear with a bang in a cloud of smoke is *weird*. Not being too keen on anything weird, the villagers took to their heels and fled.

Sharla-Tana laughed out loud. Then he waved a little black stick in the air, and the villagers found themselves struggling and kicking in a large net that had come from nowhere and had dropped right over them.

They soon discovered that struggling was no use. The net had become so entangled with their arms and legs that they could not move.

Sharla-Tana waved his little black stick again, and, just like the flowers (but without a puff of smoke), the net disappeared. Suddenly freed, the villagers tumbled and rolled on the grass.

Then they sat up and began to laugh. Sharla-Tana had started to pull a brightly-coloured flag from a small pocket in his tunic. He pulled and pulled, and then pulled again, and still the cloth kept coming. Eventually he reached the end, and he waved a huge flag of Vàldovar above his head.

The villagers cheered at the sight of the flag. Then they scratched their heads and wondered. How could Sharla-Tana have had something so large in a pocket that was so small? It was just not possible. There could only be one answer – *magic*!

What had he said in his song? He had said that he was 'Bringing *magic* spells and potions,' and he had sung of 'All the wonders of the *magic* that I bring from Araby.'

Well, that proved it, the villagers said to each other. Sharla-Tana must be a *Magician*.

Whilst the villagers had been thinking these things,

Sharla-Tana had not spoken. Now, however, he held up his hand for silence.

'My dear folk of Vàldovar,' he said, in his deep, rich voice. 'I come to you from a land that lies far, far away across the sea, and I bring you many wonderful things. Things you have never seen before. Things of which you have never even dreamed. Things, my friends, of great magic.'

He put his hand into a yellow silken pouch that hung from a cord around his waist, and drew from it a small silver chain on which was threaded a tiny, purple bead. He held it up for all to see.

'You have only to place this magic bracelet on the wrist of your left arm,' he said, 'and you will no longer feel worried or anxious.'

'That's the very thing I need,' called out Aramand the Shepherd. 'I am always worried that my sheep will stray, and I am always anxious about herding them safely home at night. May I buy it?'

'Most certainly,' said Sharla-Tana. 'For only one gold crown.'

Aramand was not a rich man. In fact, one gold crown was all the money that he had in the world. 'Still,' he thought to himself, 'this magic necklace will make my life very happy,' and so he gave the gold crown to Sharla-Tana, who slipped it into his tunic pocket.

'Here,' said Sharla-Tana, handing the bracelet to Aramand, 'it is yours.'

Aramand took the bracelet and placed it on the wrist of his left hand. Immediately, a broad smile broke out on Aramand's face. 'It works!' he cried. 'The bracelet really works. As soon as I put on the bracelet all my worries just seemed to fade away.'

Hearing this, the rest of the villagers crowded round Sharla-Tana, holding out gold crowns. And Sharla-Tana pulled bracelet after bracelet from his silken pouch, and slipped gold crown after gold crown into his tunic pocket.

There was, however, one villager who did not buy a bracelet. His name was Theodosius, and he was the Mayor of the village. Theodosius watched the villagers pressing forward, holding out their gold crowns to purchase Sharla-Tana's bracelets, and he thought to himself: 'My fellow villagers can ill afford to spend a gold crown. Their hard-earned money would be far better used to purchase shoes for their children, or food for their table.'

When Sharla-Tana had sold bracelets to all those who wished to buy them, he next drew from his tunic a small bottle. After first taking out the stopper, he turned the bottle upside down and shook from it a few drops of green liquid into his hand.

'This,' he announced to the watching villagers, 'is a magic lotion. It is made to a secret recipe created over a thousand years ago by the Queen of the Sabæans – known to some as the Queen of Sheba – whose great beauty never faded throughout her entire life. The secret of the recipe was told by the great Queen to the magicians of Araby, and today I bring it to you. Any lady who takes just a little of this lotion, and then rubs it gently into her skin, will not only gain in beauty, but will *never* grow old.'

The villagers gasped in amazement.

'I'll buy of bottle,' called out a very old woman, who had a crooked nose, teeth that stuck out, and a whiskery chin.

'You'll need to buy *two* bottles!' someone shouted, and everyone laughed.

'For just two gold crowns, this magic potion can be yours,' said Sharla-Tana, and soon he was handing out bottles to all the women of the village, and pushing more and more gold crowns into his tunic pocket (which by now was bulging with coins).

Theodosius the Mayor watched for a few more moments, then he turned and hurried away. Quickly, he saddled his small grey pony and rode, as fast as he could, to the royal castle of Vàldovar, where he asked to speak to King Ferdinand the Thirteenth.

He was shown immediately into the great hall where King Ferdinand sat upon his golden throne. On the floor around him two squirrels, three badgers and a hare were playing.

(They had just dropped in to the palace to say hello to King Ferdinand.)

'Greetings, Mayor Theodosius,' said the King. 'It is always a great pleasure to have you visit me in my castle. How may I help you, my old friend?'

Theodosius told King Ferdinand of the arrival of Sharla-Tana in his wonderful yellow balloon, with its red and orange patterns, and how the strangely-clad visitor to Vàldovar had convinced the people of the village that he was a great magician.

'And now,' Theodosius continued, 'everyone is buying magic bracelets and magic lotions from him. They are spending all their money, and they are not rich people.'

King Ferdinand listened to what Theodosius had to say, and then he thought very hard. 'This is a strange tale,' he said at last. 'It seems to me that this man, Sharla-Tana, has used a few tricks to dazzle the people of your village, in order to convince them that he is a magician. I think that we should go to seek the advice of a *true* magician. So come with me, my friend, and together we shall ride to the Wood of Wishing, there to speak to the Wizard-who-lives-in-the-Wood.'

King Ferdinand commanded that horses be made ready for himself and Theodosius. Soon they set off, and, after riding for two days and two nights, they reached the edge of the great Wood of Wishing.

Their entry into the wood was blocked, however, by bushes of Stinging Thorn, which grew so closely together that not even a mouse could squeeze between them.

King Ferdinand drew his sword, waved it in the air above his head, and called out:

Wood of Wishing, brown and green,
Guardian of the ways between
Thy towering trees – release thy spell!
No longer thy true King repel.

Then he spoke the magic word (quietly, so that Theodosius would not hear it, because the magic word is known only to the Kings of Vàldovar and to few others). As soon as the magic word had been uttered, the bushes of Stinging Thorn moved aside, and a gap opened between them that was wide enough to allow King Ferdinand and Theodosius to pass.

They rode into the wood until they came at last to a clearing in the very centre. There stood an ancient oak tree in which was set a great carved door. King Ferdinand knocked upon the door.

'It is I, King Ferdinand the Thirteenth!' he called out. 'I, and Mayor Theodosius, would speak with you, great Wizard.'

From inside the door there was a rattling of chains being

unhooked and of large, iron keys being turned in locks. Eventually, with a creaking and groaning of rusty hinges, the huge carved door opened, and out stepped the Wizard-who-lives-in-the-Wood.

The Wizard rubbed his eyes and blinked in the sunlight. 'King Ferdinand the Thirteenth,' he growled, 'this really is *too* much. I have been casting spells and making all sorts of magic all day long. Do you know how tiring that can be? No, of course you don't. Well, it *is* – and all I want to do now is go to bed and have a good long sleep. And now, here you are again, banging on my door.'

King Ferdinand and Mayor Theodosius bowed. 'We are truly sorry to disturb your sleep, ancient Wizard,' said the King, 'but we come to seek your advice concerning a visitor to Vàldovar who claims to be a magician.'

At this, the Wizard opened his eyes wide, and all signs of sleepiness fled.

'A *magician*?' he exclaimed. 'In Vàldovar? Come, King Ferdinand, and tell me quickly about this stranger. How is he called?'

'He says that his name is Sharla-Tana,' replied the King.

The Wizard began to smile. 'Well, well!' he laughed, 'so Sharla-Tana has finally found his way to Vàldovar, has he?'

'You know of this man?' asked King Ferdinand in surprise.

'Oh, yes,' replied the Wizard, 'every true Wizard knows of Sharla-Tana. He is no magician. He is a *conjuror*, an entertainer – that is all. He is no more than a performer of tricks, and he uses these tricks to persuade simple folk that he has magic powers. Then he sells them all kinds of useless things.'

'But,' said Theodosius, 'when Aramand the Shepherd put on the magic bracelet, he said that it worked and that all his worries disappeared.'

'Of course,' said the Wizard. 'Aramand *wanted* the bracelet to be magic, and so he persuaded himself that it had worked.'

'Well, what can we do?' asked King Ferdinand. 'Sharla-Tana will go to every village in Vàldovar and trick everyone into giving him money.'

'There is only one thing to be done,' the Wizard replied. He reached into the folds of his robe and took out a white magic wand and handed it to King Ferdinand. 'Give this wand to Sharla-Tana, and say that it is a present from you, the King, to thank Sharla-Tana for bringing his magic to Vàldovar. Tell him that the wand will not work its magic unless he first taps himself with it three times on his forehead.'

King Ferdinand and Theodosius thanked the Wizard-who-lives-in-the-Wood, and, bearing the white magic wand, returned to the King's castle.

They arrived to find Sharla-Tana standing just outside the castle, beside his balloon. Around him stood a large crowd of people. Sharla-Tana was pulling gaily-coloured birds out of people's ears; the birds would then fly up into the sky and suddenly disappear with a bright flash. He changed a small bunch of flowers into a large frog that hopped away towards the pond in the castle gardens. Then, from the tall white hat worn by Cristolf the Baker, he pulled out a wriggling little rabbit.

In between his tricks, he sold all kinds of things to the people in the crowd, who bought everything that he showed them. There were jars of magic ointment for soothing aching feet, sticks of firewood that would never stop burning, cups that kept filling themselves with a delicious, cool drink, and many other wonders.

'Master Magician,' called the King, striding forward. 'I welcome you to Vàldovar, and I thank you for having brought your magic powers to our small country.'

Sharla-Tana beamed. 'Thank you, your Majesty,' he replied. 'I have many wonderful things that your people are eager to purchase from me.'

King Ferdinand then gave the white magic wand to Sharla-Tana. 'This magic wand,' said the King, ' is a gift from me and from the people of Vàldovar. To release its magic powers, you must tap yourself with it three times on your forehead.'

Now (as the Wizard-who-lives-in-the-Wood knew)

Sharla-Tana was not a *real* magician. He simply performed tricks to make people *think* he was a magician, so that they would then buy his bracelets and potions. But (or so he thought) with a truly magic wand, he would be able to work *real* magic, and he would be able to impress the people even more. So he took the wand eagerly, and tapped his forehead with it three times.

Then, the strangest thing happened. The wand leaped from Sharla-Tana's hand and flew round and round him. As it did so, it kept poking him – first on his nose, then his arms, then his back, his knees, then all over his body.

Sharla-Tana yelped and danced about, waving his arms, trying to make the wand go away. But it was no use. The wand continued poking and prodding. As it did so, the wand sang in a clear, high voice. This is what it said.

To wield a wand of magic,
Remember this condition –
The outcome will be tragic
If you're not a real Magician!

A magic wand won't aid you
If there is a suspicion
That tricks alone have made you
Look like a true Magician.

If from the words you've spoken
The truth was an omission,
The golden rule you've broken
Of Wizard and Magician.

So you who from the East came,
Consider your position,
*And tell us if you **now** claim,*
To be a great Magician.

Or torment will continue –
I'll prod with repetition,
Until you find it in you
To say you're no Magician.

Sharla-Tana was so surprised, that he fell flat on his back. As he did so, his scarlet cloak flew up, and all kinds of things fell from beneath it. There was a rabbit, two brightly-coloured birds, a large flag, a frog, and a small packet which immediately burst open and turned into an enormous bunch of flowers.

'Look!' shouted Aethrid the Watchman, 'those are the things that Sharla-Tana makes appear. They were hidden under his cloak, all the time. He is *not* a magician at all. He can't make real magic – he just does tricks.'

'And his bracelet doesn't work, either,' called out

Aramand the Shepherd. 'I *still* worry about my sheep.' Aramand took off the bracelet that he had bought and threw it down on the ground.

The old woman with the crooked nose, teeth that stuck out, and a whiskery chin, said: 'The two bottles of lotion that he sold me are no use either. I've rubbed and rubbed it into my skin, but it hasn't made me beautiful, as he promised it would. In fact, it has made me go cross-eyed.'

Sharla-Tana realized that his secret had been discovered, and he scrambled to his feet, the magic wand now lying lifeless at his feet.

'Sharla-Tana,' said King Ferdinand severely, 'what have you to say? The wand has shown that you are a trickster, and not a magician. You have taken much money from these good people, for things that do not work. Surely you must be ashamed of yourself.'

Sharla-Tana hung his head. 'Indeed I am, your Majesty,' he said.

'Then what do you think you ought to do to make amends to those whom you have tricked and cheated?' the King asked.

Sharla-Tana thought for a moment, and then he said: 'I shall return all the money that was given to me. But more than this, I shall – with your permission – remain here in the fair land of Vàldovar to entertain the people with my skills in performing magic tricks. Never again shall I claim to be a magician. I shall call myself Sharla-Tana the *Conjuror*.'

King Ferdinand smiled. 'Then, Sharla-Tana,' he said, 'so be it.'

And so that is just what Sharla-Tana did. He remained all his life in Vàldovar, and travelled far and wide throughout that country. He was much in demand as an entertainer at birthday parties, where he amazed everyone by pulling rabbits out of hats, finding coins behind people's ears, and making all kinds of things appear in the most unlikely places, only to disappear a few moments later with a flash and puff of smoke. Even though everyone knew that these were just tricks, and that Sharla-Tana was not really a magician, they had to admit that he did the tricks very well.

Thus it was that Sharla-Tana the Conjuror became a well-loved citizen of Vàldovar. Even today, the Valdovarians talk about the stranger who came from a far-off land, arriving across the sea in a basket suspended beneath a wonderful, coloured balloon, and who stayed to become the most famous conjuror that Vàldovar has ever known.

Back in the Wood of Wishing, a brightly coloured bird flew down into the clearing where stood the Wizard-who-lives-in-the-Wood. The Wizard held out his hand, and the little bird alighted on it. (It was one of the birds that, during his performances, Sharla-Tana kept under his cloak, later producing it with a flourish from a lady's hat or a gentleman's tunic pocket.)

The little bird cheeped and chirped, and told the Wizard how the magic wand had caused Sharla-Tana to fall over, and how all the things he used to perform his magic tricks had fallen from beneath his cloak.

When the bird had finished telling its story, it flew up into the air, and returned to Sharla-Tana (because it enjoyed being part of his magic act).

The Wizard laughed when he thought about what the little bird had told him. 'I think,' he said to himself, 'that one person making magic is quite enough for a small country like Vàldovar!'

Then, still laughing, the Wizard-who-lives-in-the-Wood turned and walked back into his home in the ancient oak. Behind him, the great carved door swung shut.

The Stonemason

ar, far away, in the little country of Vàldovar, by a stream of cool, clear water running through a meadow ablaze with wild flowers, there stands a pile of rocks and stones. What is so remarkable is that every rock and every stone is very, very beautiful. Some are red, others blue or green or orange; some have swirly markings of many different colours; in some there is the glint of crystals.

Every day, two or three Valdovarians come and polish every single stone, and then place each back carefully onto the pile. At the foot of the pile of stones stands a small plaque of pink marble on which is written:

> *These stones lie here*
> *In memory of*
> *Gregorius the Stonemason*
> *Who lived many, many years ago.*

In this story I shall tell you all about Gregorius, and you will come to understand why, even today, the people of

Vàldovar still speak of him, and why they do honour to the stones.

The tiny country of Vàldovar is very beautiful. If you were to go there (which would actually be rather difficult because – as you know – Vàldovar does not appear on any map), you would see many wonderful things: great mountains covered all year long with snow; deep forests where deer roam between majestic, ancient trees; wide, golden beaches; and sweeping green meadows, filled with flowers of all colours.

You can well understand, then, why the people of Vàldovar love their country, and why they always try their hardest to preserve its beauty. They *never* drop any litter on the streets or in the fields, and they make sure that their houses are always kept neat and clean, with roses and other climbing flowers growing around the doors and windows.

Once, however, there was one Valdovarian to whom the beauty of the country meant little. This was a man whose name was Gregorius. Gregorius was a Stonemason (that is someone who works with the stone used to make and mend walls, or to build houses and bridges).

Better than anyone else in Vàldovar, Gregorius knew the ways of stone. He could take a rock of any form, no matter how uneven or knobbly it might be, and, in hardly any time at all, he could shape it into a perfect fit for a wall or a bridge.

Gregorius thought of nothing but stone. Whenever he

walked in the fields he never noticed the flowers or trees, and did not look up at the sky or at the gaily coloured birds. He did not smell the sweet scent of the Honeyflower bushes, or hear the buzzing of the bees as they flitted from flower to flower. The warmth of the sun on his face, the caress of the breeze on his arms, the fleeting shadows cast upon the meadows by the fleecy clouds – all these things passed unnoticed.

Although all the maidens in the villages of Vàldovar thought that he was very handsome, Gregorius had no eyes for them. Instead, he kept his gaze fixed firmly upon the ground, looking for stones. When he saw one that he thought to be of an interesting colour or shape, he would pick it up and put it in a little pouch that hung from a belt around his waist.

As he did so, he would hum a little song to himself:

I tread the country path alone,
To find a stone, a shiny stone.
And if perchance my foot should knock
Against a rock, a rugged rock,
I stoop to gaze upon its form,
My heart to warm, my soul to warm.
Aught else that in the world may be
I do not see, I cannot see.
Oh, rocks and stones the world do make,
I love them all. My breath they take!

Small and smooth, or large and rough,
To touch them is for me enough.
I do not think that I shall see
A sight that warms the heart of me,
As much as granite, limestone, shale –
All other things to me seem pale.
Show me not wood, nor cloth, nor bone,
For all I wish to see is – stone.

Gregorius the Stonemason lived all alone in a small house beside a pretty stream. One day, he said to himself: 'I think my house is rather too small. I have gathered so many stones and rocks during my walks around Vàldovar that I can use them to build myself a new house on the other side of the stream.'

And that is what he did. Day after day he worked, putting one stone upon another and one rock upon another. So cleverly did he place the stones that they fitted each other perfectly, and needed no mortar to hold them together.

At last, the new house was built. Gregorius stood back to admire it, and decided that it was the most wonderful house he had ever seen. He was, however, the only person in Vàldovar to think so.

When the other Valdovarians came to look at what Gregorius had built, their mouths fell open in horror. The house was not only very big – it was also the *ugliest* house that anyone had ever seen. And it certainly did not fit in at all with the green meadow and pretty stream.

When they told Gregorius what they thought, he simply smiled and shook his head.

'Just look at these interesting stones,' he said, pointing to the walls and roof of his house. 'See how hard they are. Look how this one is bright and that one dull; how this one is smooth and that one jagged and rough.'

'But the house is so *ugly*,' protested the others. 'It quite spoils the beauty of the meadow. And just look how it hides the stream. Don't you think that it would be much nicer to be able to look at the silver, rippling water in the stream than at the dull, boring old stones in the walls of your house?'

Then the people begged him: 'Won't you please pull it down and restore the beauty of the meadow and stream?'

Gregorius looked around him in surprise. 'I see no beauty in grass or water,' he said, 'but only in stone. The meadow and the stream mean nothing to me.' And so the house remained standing.

The Valdovarians were greatly distressed. They could not understand how Gregorius could build a house that was so hideous to look at.

'But what can we do,' said Cristolf the Baker, 'if Gregorius cannot see how he has spoiled the countryside?'

'Well, we should certainly tell King Ferdinand about it,'

said Leofwin the Forester. 'Perhaps he can command Gregorius to take down his horrible house.'

And so they all went to the royal palace where King Ferdinand the Thirteenth received them in the great hall. King Ferdinand sat upon his golden throne, stroking a fox that had wandered in from the garden. (All the animals in Vàldovar knew King Ferdinand; he was always so kind and gentle with them that they often just popped in to see him.)

King Ferdinand greeted his subjects. 'And how can I help you today?' he asked.

Oriel the Flower Lady explained how Gregorius had used his collection of rocks and stones to build a big house in the pretty meadow, right by the stream.

'Gregorius is quite unable to see that his new house is dreadful to look at,' she said, 'and we cannot make him understand how it destroys the beauty of that place.'

'And so,' added Ranulf the Gardener, 'we wondered whether you could command him to pull the house down.'

King Ferdinand stroked his chin and thought. 'Well, now,' he said at last, 'I don't think that it would be right for me to do that. You see, although Gregorius does not appreciate the beauty of the flowers or the stream, or of the trees and sky, he *does* find beauty in stones. How can I ask him to destroy that which *to him* is beautiful?' King Ferdinand reminded his subjects of an old Valdovarian song:

Some say that there's beauty in winter,
And others see beauty in spring;
The fool can see beauty in nothing,
The wise man in everything.

We think that we know what is beauty,
But later (as we become older),
We see that all beauty resides in
The eye of the beauty's beholder.

If others your world would remodel,
Say not that all beauty is gone;
Rejoice that these others see beauty
Where fools would declare there is none.

The Valdovarians realized that their King spoke the truth. Gregorius found his stones beautiful and so *to him* his new house was also a thing of beauty. It would be cruel to make him pull the house down.

Then, King Ferdinand spoke again: 'I feel sorry for Gregorius the Stonemason,' he said, 'because he sees the beauty *only* of stones. I should like to show him that there is beauty, too, in the countryside and in the many other wonderful things that are in the world.'

'Perhaps the Wizard-who-lives-in-the-Wood may be able

to help him,' suggested Oriel the Flower Lady.

'Yes, perhaps he may,' King Ferdinand agreed. 'I shall go forthwith and seek his advice.'

The King's swiftest horse was saddled and made ready for the journey, and King Ferdinand rode for two days and two nights, coming at last to the edge of the ancient Wood of Wishing. The King's entry into the wood was, however, barred by the criss-crossed branches of trees. Drawing his sword, and holding it high above his head, King Ferdinand called out:

Wood of Wishing, trees that hear,
I – King Ferdinand – draw near.
As sovereign of this ancient land,
I bid you bow to my command.

He then spoke the magic word. I cannot tell you what that word is, for it is known only to the Kings of Vàldovar and to few others. When the trees heard the magic word, they slowly raised their branches, with a creaking, cracking sound, and King Ferdinand was able to pass beneath them.

He rode swiftly down a leafy path to a clearing in the very centre of the wood. There stood a mighty oak, in the huge trunk of which was set a great, carved door. Before the door stood the Wizard-who-lives-in-the-Wood. The silver stars on the Wizard's long, blue robe twinkled. The blue moons on his tall, white, pointed hat flickered with a strange light.

'I greet you, Master Wizard,' called King Ferdinand, dismounting from his horse.

The Wizard stroked his long, white beard, and pointed his wooden staff at the King. 'So many times have you spoken the magic word, King Ferdinand, that my trees complain that they cannot sleep peacefully. They find it exhausting to have to keep lifting their branches or swaying to one side so that you may pass into the wood.'

The King bowed. 'I beg forgiveness of your trees, mighty Wizard,' he replied, 'but I come again to seek your advice about a matter of importance.'

The Wizard nodded. 'So speak, King Ferdinand,' he said. 'Tell me what now troubles the fair land of Vàldovar.'

King Ferdinand explained how Gregorius the Stone-mason saw beauty only in stones and rocks, and how he had spoiled the countryside by building his ugly stone house.

'I cannot command Gregorius to pull down his house,' said the King, 'for to him it is a thing of wonder and delight. Yet, if he were able to see the beauty of things *other* than stones and rocks, I am sure that he would understand why his fellow Valdovarians feel that his house spoils the countryside.'

The Wizard continued to stroke his long, white beard, as he thought very hard. 'Yes,' he said at last, 'this is indeed a most serious matter.'

Then he smiled. 'I know exactly what you must do. Listen carefully. You must command Gregorius the Stonemason to undertake a journey to the Grey Cliffs, which stand at the foot of the Eastern Mountains. Tell him that you wish to know whether the rock of which the cliffs are made could be used to build a castle for Prince Almeric and Princess Britta.'

'I do not understand how this will change Gregorius's ideas about what is beautiful and what is not,' said King Ferdinand.

'Patience,' replied the Wizard. 'There is more that you need to do. Tell Gregorius that he must take with him food and water, for he will find little to eat and drink when he reaches the Grey Cliffs. To carry his water, he should use this.' And, reaching into the folds of his cloak, the Wizard drew forth a flagon made of brown leather. Then the Wizard took a small knife and with it pierced a small hole in the base of the flagon.

Though King Ferdinand was still puzzled and could not see how telling Gregorius to go to the Grey Cliffs with a leaking water-flagon could possibly solve the problem, he nevertheless thanked the Wizard warmly and returned to the royal castle.

Once there, he summoned Gregorius and bade him ride to the Grey Cliffs in the Eastern Mountains.

'You know everything there is to know about rocks,' said the King. 'I wish you to tell me whether the rock of the Grey

Cliffs could be used to make a fine castle for Prince Almeric and Princess Britta.'

Gregorius bowed. 'It shall be done, your Majesty,' he said.

'And take with you this flagon,' said the King. 'In the Eastern Mountains there is little to be found to eat or to drink, and so you must carry with you food and this flagon filled with water.' The King did not tell Gregorius how the Wizard had pierced the flagon with his knife.

Thanking the King, Gregorius accepted the leather flagon, and then set out immediately to do the King's bidding.

The journey was long, and it took Gregorius six days to reach the Eastern Mountains. At last, he stood before the Grey Cliffs that rose up, tall and magnificent, before him.

Gregorius spent many hours examining the rock of the Cliffs. He used a small silver hammer to break off little pieces of rock, and these he popped into his pouch.

As the day wore on, Gregorius started to feel hungry and thirsty, and so he took down from his horse the basket containing his food, and the leather water flagon. Sitting on a rock, he pulled the stopper out of the flagon, raised the flagon to his lips, and started to drink – but it was *empty*! (And, of course, we know why – don't we?)

Gregorius turned the flagon upside down and shook it, but not a single drop of water remained in it. He was *sure* that he'd filled it up only that morning, from a small stream of clear water. He looked carefully at the flagon, but so cleverly had the Wizard pierced it with his knife, that Gregorius could see no sign of a hole in it.

Gregorius scratched his head. What was he to do? He was really very thirsty and he just *had* to find some water.

He decided to look around to see whether he might discover a small stream or pool. He searched everywhere, but could find no trace of water.

Eventually, he came across the mouth of a small cave, set into the foot of the Grey Cliffs. It was very dark inside. Peering into the cave, Gregorius thought that he could hear, very faintly, the sound of water. 'Ah!' he said, 'I may be able to fill my flagon with fresh, cool water.'

Cautiously, he entered the cave and, with one hand on the wall and the other hand held out in front of him, he advanced into the darkness. The further he went into the cave, the louder the sound of rushing water became.

Then he saw a light ahead of him and he realized that the cave must have another opening. He hurried forward until, at last, he came out of the cave into bright sunlight.

Gregorius gasped in amazement at the scene before him. He found himself in a small, secret valley, surrounded on all sides by steep cliffs. The rocky floor of the valley was covered in soft green moss, and here and there were brightly coloured flowers. Tall trees reached up towards the sky, their leaves dappling the golden sunlight. Cream-coloured doves swooped and cooed in the still air.

The greatest wonder, however, lay before him. Cascading down from the highest cliff, a great waterfall fell into a deep pool. Then, from the pool, there flowed a stream of clear, cool water which tumbled and bubbled over rocky outcrops.

The stream was spanned by a small bridge, and Gregorius was astonished to see, standing in the middle of the bridge, a beautiful Lady, clad in a gown of silver and gold. There were flowers in her hair.

In her hand, the Lady carried a crystal goblet filled with water from the stream. She held out the goblet towards Gregorius and, with her other hand, beckoned to him to join her on the bridge.

As he walked forward, Gregorius heard the Lady singing in a clear, sweet voice:

This is my secret valley,
Where flows the crystal stream
'Twixt mossy banks and flowers.
Come stand with me and dream
Of cooling, soothing waters
That fall from high above.
Come stand with me and dream, I pray,
Of beauty and of love.

My cup with water brimming
I give to thee to drink,
To ease thy thirsty spirit.
Come stand with me and think
Of trees that scatter sunlight,
And gently cooing dove.
Come stand with me and think, I pray,
Of beauty and of love.

I call to thee to join me
Where waters pass below.
My hand I reach towards thee.
Come stand with me and know
The world is full of wonders –
Both earth and sky above.
Come stand with me and know, I pray,
Of beauty and of love.

Gregorius stood by the Lady on the little bridge. He took the goblet that was offered to him and drank. It was the most wonderful water he had ever tasted, and after only one small sip his thirst was instantly quenched.

Suddenly, he realized that, from the time that he had emerged from the cave into the secret valley, he had not *once* thought about stones or rocks. He had eyes only for the waterfall, the trees, the moss and the flowers, for the bridge and the swirling stream below it – but, most of all, for the beautiful Lady in the gold and silver gown.

The Lady held Gregorius's hand and spoke to him: 'Look around you, Gregorius Stonemason, and tell me what you see.'

'I see only beauty, Lady,' Gregorius replied.

'That,' said the Lady, 'is my gift to you.' Then she reached out her hand and touched Gregorius on his brow.

At once, the valley disappeared. The waterfall and stream, the bridge, the trees, the mossy valley floor, the bright flowers, and the creamy doves, were there no more.

Gregorius found himself standing once again at the foot of the Grey Cliffs. Of the cave there was no sign.

But *something* had changed. Where Gregorius had once seen only rocks and stones, he now saw the plants that grew everywhere, and he saw and heard the birds flitting between the trees and bushes. He saw the sky with its fleecy clouds. He felt the cool breeze upon his face. And he found it *all* beautiful!

And, what is more, Gregorius noticed that, in his hand, he still held the crystal goblet that the Lady had given to him.

When, six days later, Gregorius arrived home, he went directly to the new house that he had built in the meadow by the little stream. He now realized its ugliness and he understood why the other Valdovarians were so upset, because he could see that it spoiled the countryside.

He thereupon seized a huge hammer and began to knock down the house, stone by stone. The sound of his hammering soon brought all the people running to see what Gregorius was doing. King Ferdinand, too, rode out from the royal castle.

Everyone was astonished to see Gregorius standing before a huge pile of rocks and stones – the ugly house had gone!

Gregorius told the King and the others that now he no longer saw beauty only in stones and rocks, but all about him. He did not tell anyone, though, of the secret valley, or of the Lady in the gold and silver gown.

'I am sorry that I spoiled the lovely countryside with my dreadful house,' Gregorius said to those gathered around the pile of rocks and stones.

But then, a very strange thing happened. Cristolf the Baker spotted something gleaming amongst the pile of stones that had once been Gregorius's house, and he stepped forward and picked up a small, shiny stone, that glinted in the sunlight.

'I had not realized,' Cristolf said, 'how beautiful a stone could be. May I have this, Gregorius?'

'Most certainly, Master Cristolf,' replied Gregorius, with a smile.

Then others, too, began to find interesting and pretty stones, and Gregorius was happy to permit his friends to keep them.

From that day on, Gregorius the Stonemason chose only

the most beautiful stones for the walls and bridges and anything else that was built in Vàldovar, and he always made sure that nothing that he did ever again spoiled the beauty of the countryside. He was also very happy that the other Valdovarians had discovered for themselves that rocks and stones are also beautiful, in their own special way.

Away from the meadow and the small stream, Gregorius built for himself a small, pretty house. This time, however, he used not only stone and rock, but many different kinds of wood. Roses grew around the door, with honeysuckle and columbine.

And inside the house, on a small table, always surrounded by fresh flowers from the meadows and woods, stood the crystal goblet that had been given to him by the Lady on the bridge.

Two cream-coloured doves flew down into the clearing that lies at the heart of the Wood of Wishing. They sat on the shoulders of the Wizard-who-lives-in-the-Wood and cooed softly into his ears.

The doves told the Wizard how Gregorius the Stonemason had found his way into the secret valley of the waterfall, how he had drunk the magic water from the crystal goblet, and how he had suddenly understood how beautiful everything in the world really was.

The Wizard smiled as the two doves flew away, up into the trees, and back to the secret valley in the Eastern Mountains.

'The Lady has truly given Gregorius the greatest gift of all,' he said. 'And, not only that, but the people of Vàldovar have discovered that even stones have a beauty of their own.'

Then, from amongst the trees, there suddenly appeared badgers and foxes, rabbits and deer, voles and woodpigeons, and many, many other wild creatures. Clustering around the Wizard's feet, they squeaked, whistled, barked, and made all the other sounds that woodland creatures make.

The Wizard listened carefully to what they said, and then he laughed. 'So, my little friends,' he said, 'you heard what the doves told me? And what is it that you want to know?'

He listened again to the animals' voices.

'Oh, you want to know who the Lady is? Well, I would have thought that you could guess her name. No? Then I shall tell you. She is the bringer of light, the spirit of the world, and the meaning of life. Before her, even the Beast kneels. Her name is *Beauty*.'

Then, still smiling, the Wizard-who-lives-in-the-Wood turned and walked back into his home in the ancient oak. Behind him, the great carved door swung shut.

The Wood of Wishing Verses

The Princess

Wood of Wishing, it is told
That thou art ruled by magic old,
Permit me to pass on my way,
When this – the Magic Word – I say.

The Sea Lady

Wood of Wishing, harken well.
Thine ancient trees, 'neath ancient spell,
That bar my path, apart must stand.
Make way for your King Ferdinand!

The Captain of the Guard

Wood of Wishing, tree and bush,
Bracken, fern, and reed and rush,
Ash and elm, and rowan tree,
Bow your heads, and welcome me.

The Cook

Wood of Wishing, hear my call;
Lower now thy leafy wall.
With the Wizard I would talk,
And down thy sylvan paths must walk.

The Conjuror

Wood of Wishing, brown and green,
Guardian of the ways between
Thy towering trees – release thy spell!
No longer thy true King repel.

The Stonemason

Wood of Wishing, trees that hear,
I – King Ferdinand – draw near.
As sovereign of this ancient land,
I bid you bow to my command.

To Dream Again of Vàldovar

Now once again my song I've sung,
And we must take our leave
Of Vàldovar, that hidden land,
But this you must believe –
The time will come when you and I
Shall visit there once more,
To meet the royal King and Queen,
And tread the leafy floor
Of woodland glade where lives the one
True Wizard in his tree;
And folk of Vàldovar we'll meet,
And wonders we shall see.
We'll walk on mighty mountains,
And in forests where still roam
The unicorns of golden mane,
And which are also home
To other creatures stranger far
Than any that now live.
My tales of these, and much, much more,
I vow to you I'll give.

So now to bed, and now to sleep,
To dream a golden dream
Of nests of stealing magpies, and
Of rings that in them gleam,
Of cooks and guards and conjurors,
And creatures of the sea,
Of princesses and stonemasons,
And you will surely be
In flowered fields of Vàldovar,
Beside its silver streams.
Once more shall tales of long ago
Come to you in your dreams.

www.kingandwizard.com